Names On The Tower

by

S.F. Brooke

1

This book is a work of historical fiction, based loosely on real people and real events. Details that cannot be historically verified are purely products of the author's imagination.

Table of Contents:

Translations of French chapter titles are the first sentence of each chapter.

Chapter One - Je n'aurais pas dû écouter

I should not have listened. Let us just say that before I continue telling you my story. As I now know, you should never eavesdrop. Never. Yet I did, and this journey was created because of that. My story is one that started accidentally. It involves good times and bad times, romance and betrayal, truth and lies. I've decided to write it down because...well someone should know it. Someone should know the truth behind some things, I mean everyone wants to have their story written right? So, let me take you back to the summer when I was seventeen years old...

✳✳✳

The punch in the face was something I should have expected, but as I spit out the metallic taste of blood, I decided that this guy was going down. I spun around and rammed my head into his stomach, slamming both of us into the dirt. The school ground was alive with cheering. The friends I had on the sidelines were shouting tips and my name. I pummeled into the guy again. He had done the wrong thing and dishonored a young lady at the school, spreading rumors and calling names. Clarisse was the loudest of the bunch. Her voice carried as I punched her assailant. He grabbed my arm and twisted us around, slamming my back into the dusty ground that we were wrestling on. I blocked the fists to my face but got a few to my ribs effectively getting the air to rush out of my lungs.

"Now you are in for it," I growled at him. His punch missed my head by centimeters and I bit his arm, using my other hand to shove at his shoulder. I sprung up from the ground. He twisted to look at me and I put up my fists like the boxers I had seen in the past. "Come on!" I shouted, throwing a punch at his big nose. It gave a satisfying crunch and at the same time, my wrist sent aches of pain down my arm. I kicked his legs out from him and he stayed down, groaning in pain as he held his hands over his nose. *"Cochon dégoûtant."* I spat, wiping blood from my face. I grabbed my newsboy hat off the ground and dusted it off. I grabbed the other boy's hat and walked towards Clarisse, bowing at the waist. "Your prize, *ma charmante dame.*" I handed her the hat, smiling as the loveliest girl I had ever known took it and nodded her head in thanks. Soon enough everyone heard teachers yelling and we scattered like rats in sunlight as two of the school's teachers headed towards us. My friends and I took off. Running was painful but getting punished would hurt more. Especially when your father is one of the teachers at the school. The three of us slowed down and finished our walks to our homes. Tomas and Val, two of my friends, congratulated me on my fighting skills, something I was known for in school, but I shook off their praise. "I was simply defending Clarisse's honor."

Clarisse laughed daintily, "*Merci,* Al." She handed me her hanky and I took it, using it to wipe off any excess blood from my face, hoping I did not bruise. I jokingly handed it back to her and she squealed to keep away from it. I loved the way my name sounded on her tongue. Inwardly I puffed out my chest in pride, but outside I simply smiled.

The year was 1887, in the illustrious city of Paris, France. The school day was released, and children of all ages were leaving the schoolhouse with excitement, milling around towards their own houses. Tomas and Val had straight, cinnamon brown hair like mine, minus the dust, and each of us was dressed in a white cotton shirt, I had my brown suspenders on, and black pants with rugged-looking mud-colored shoes. I always wore mine out from my job as an apprentice, which involved a lot of running. At seventeen my friends and I were finishing out last year of schooling, then would look for jobs or apprenticeships around town. Clarisse was sixteen. She was *magnifique,* beautiful, and had striking cobalt blue eyes that seemed to stare through people. The four of us had been friends for a long time. Val, Tomas, and I saw each other every day

6

while we only saw Clarisse whenever she could get away from her mother. Clarisse had finished her schooling years ago. The day was hot, and I was sweating through my shirt. We walked across the dirt road, the gravel crunching under our feet. I looked over at Clarisse and winced at how hot her dress looked, but her bonnet was protecting her face at least from the harsh sunlight.

"Aleron!" I heard my father call, I stopped where I was walking and quickly said goodbye to my friends. I clutched my newsboy hat to my head and took off towards my father. He was a teacher at our school. He held an honorable position on the board and his strict schedule made skipping school a challenge.

"Yes, Father?" I replied, pulling up short to stop myself from running into him.

"*Dieu merci*, Aleron.", My father said, his voice filled with frustration. I wondered what he'd meant. Was it the fact that I had gotten into another fight or the fact that I missed two days of school this week alone? Turns out it was the latter, "When I asked you if you were going to school you said yes, didn't you?" My father asked.

I nodded. "Yes, I did but..."

My father cut me off. "So, you knew that you only needed to come to my class? Yes or no?" His brown eyes were angry, and I frowned at the disappointed look on his face.

"Yes..." I eventually said, putting my head down.

I heard my father sigh, grabbing papers and his books in his arms. "I do not need this stress right now Al. Your uncle is coming to stay with us this week and I need you to be on your best behavior." He grabbed my arm and we headed out towards home.

7

I bit my lip in thought. My uncle was an astronomer and a mathematician. My father's older brother was coming into town because of the construction of Gustave Eiffel's latest progress. It was rumored to be called the Eiffel Tower and was set to be finished with construction by the time the 1889 World's Fair came to Paris. He was planning on staying with us and I was more than excited to learn about his travels and for him to teach me about the study of the stars.

"I'm sorry." I ended up saying lamely.

We walked in silence and the gravel crunching was the loudest thing that I heard. Our home was actually near the construction site of *Monsieur* Eiffel's project and it was alive with activity as men yelled in French and English. I stopped and stared for a moment as my father walked on ahead of me. Gustave Eiffel was the topic of controversy in the whole of France right now. The Tower had been drawing criticism from several people, many who were trying to stop the building entirely. Gustave Eiffel was trying to accomplish a feat that no one had tried to do before! The Tower was going to be the tallest building in Paris France, standing at three hundred meters tall. I don't know if the man was stupid or he was a genius to try to pull it off, but I liked that he was willing to try it. It came to a head when a Committee of Three Hundred was formed, a member for every meter of the Tower's height. As an apprentice for an architect, I loved to learn and create and build. My father called me, and I tore my gaze away from the movements of the men working to create something I only dreamed to be a part of.

I arrived at home and started getting my uncle's room ready, while my father prepared dinner for both of us. He would be coming on the next train.

***

The following day my father and I went to greet my Uncle François Aragon. We met at his station platform. The train whistles were loud and startled me enough that I was snapped out of my thoughts.

"Aleron, Jacques!" My uncle shouted joyfully as he stepped off the train. He had a grin on his long face. His black hair shining in the morning sun made him look older than I last remembered him to be; almost eleven years ago before my mother died. She was my father's best friend and her brother-in-law's closest confidant, losing her to cholera was a blow to both of them. I was only six when she died, but I remember her face which always had a smile on it. She smelled like cinnamon and her hugs were a warmth I'd been missing every day she'd been gone. I'd inherited her smile and the same brown hair. I wondered if my uncle saw her in me when he saw me all grown up. I hugged him, and he clapped my back a few times, almost roughly.

He took off my hat and ruffled my hair. "Look at you. All grown up."

I grinned and jokingly pushed myself away from him, smoothing down my hair. "Could say the same for you Uncle."

I put my hat back on and grabbed my uncle's luggage, letting my father and him reconnect as I walked behind them. Being raised in a way that eavesdropping was looked down upon I only heard snippets of what they were talking about but mostly kept to myself. My uncle settled into the room that my father and I had set up and we ate dinner together talking about his travels and studies. This is when the topic of the Tower came up.

9

"So, what do you two think about that crazy lunatic Eiffel and his grand schemed project?" My uncle asked.

I waited to hear my father's answer.

"I think there's something ingenious in the man but also a bit of insanity in his way of thinking," He ended up saying after some thought and careful choosing of his words.

I nodded along with my father. "I think the same. It is going to be an incredible feat if he pulls it off, but I think that it will take him longer than the amount of time he has given himself. Imagine if he does it though! It would be amazing!" I gushed, my excitement of the prospect of having something as spectacular as Eiffel's latest project in the middle of my town.

The two other men at the table laughed at me for their amusement. "Well, Francois you can see what your nephew thinks about Gustave Eiffel."

My uncle laughed and I could tell that it was slightly forced. Clearly, we did not agree with our opinions about *Monsieur* Eiffel. We finished dinner and after we cleared the dishes my father told me to head to my room.

"But *père,* I wanted to talk to Uncle," I objected.

My father gently shook his head and motioned for me to head to my room. "Your uncle and I need to talk about something important that children don't need to hear."

"I'm not a child," I pointed out, bristling a little, but my father gave me a pointed look.

I relented, not wanting an argument, but I wanted to hear their conversation. I waited until my uncle and father headed into the study then tiptoed out to press my ear against the door. I knew that if I got caught, I would be grounded for life, but I went with it anyway. Their voices were hushed, and I strained to hear anything they were saying.

I barely heard what my father said at the end of his sentence as they were whispering. "What?! Francois that's crazy!"

My uncle's voice was demanding and concerned all at once. "Tell me differently Jacques, the man brought it upon himself! There are people that dislike him. There have been rumors like this for ages. Gustave Eiffel is going to be murdered, and it will happen before the World's Fair opens."

I shot up from my spot, crouched near the door, a gasp of astonishment leaving my lips. I slapped a hand over my mouth and hurried into my room. My mind was swirling, and my thoughts were churning. Gustave Eiffel, the genius, the mad man, was going to be *killed?* It seemed impossible.

Chapter Two - Des Erreurs Ont été Commises

Mistakes were made, I realized, as I stared up at my ceiling that night. My uncle's words were ringing through my head like Notre Dame's church bells. Someone was plotting to kill *Monsieur* Eiffel? I could not believe it. I should not have eavesdropped but now that the information was stuck in my head it would not get out. That night in bed was filled with lots of tossing and turning. My dreams went on wild escapades of theories that started filling my mind.

The next morning, I was groggy, but I made my way to school anyway. The sun was rising, taking the chilly fog from the air, and the ground was damp as I walked into the schoolhouse. I sat on the bench in the back waiting for my two friends, Tomas and Val, to join me. The teacher was an older man with lines on his face that looked like the roads on maps of the town. Their many paths were deep, and he looked tired of his job, possibly of life in general. *Monsieur* Ennuyeux was his name and as he rang the bell, the other kids came trickling in, their voices loud and annoying. There were kids of all ages since we were all taught in the same room. We ranged from six and seven years old to my own age of seventeen. Most of the kids were boys which may have made the group even rowdier. As class began, the teacher was talking about simple math, his mustache moving more than his actual lips did, and I nudged Val's elbow.

"I have something to tell you after school. Pass it on," I whispered under my breath, not taking my head up from the math problems on my blackboard in front of me. The sounds of chalk scraping against the board made my ears ache. Val nodded and passed it on to Tomas who was sitting on the opposite side of Val.

"What is it about?" Val whispered next to me.

"I will tell you later. We have to get Clarisse too," I replied. We were all startled when a ruler came slamming down near our desks.

"*Monsieurs*. That will be enough talking," Our teacher scolded, his face stern.

"Yes, sir," the three of us replied in unison, turning our attention back to the math. The teacher walked away; his watchful eye put on some other poor subject

"Meet at our spot. The park near my house," I mumbled out of the side of my mouth, hoping Val heard it.

"*Oui,*" He replied.

The school day dragged on and I couldn't wait for it to end. When it finally ended, around noon, my friends and I shot out of the building, running to Clarisse's house. I held onto my newsboy hat as the dusty wind picked up from my friends' feet. The three of us stood in front of Clarisse's house, noticing that her mother was in the living room with her. Tomas, Val, and I scurried under one of their windows like rabbits being chased. We pulled up when we got to another window that was closer to Clarisse. Val handed me a handful of dirt and I threw it at the window causing the small pebbles to clink off the glass. We did this two more times before Clarisse came to the window and opened it.

"What are you three *imbéciles*doing here?!", She whisper-yelled, her blue eyes looking over her shoulder. "If my mother catches me…" She trailed off before turning her gaze back to us.

Clarisse never failed to make my heart stutter. Her face was round and perfect... her lips full, and her blue eyes were... oh so captivating. The blue dress she was wearing only enhanced their color. Her brown hair was thrown lazily over her shoulder. It was one of the few times her bonnet was not covering the soft waves of her hair.

"Aleron!" Clarisse yelled at me, frustration crossing over her face. "What are you doing here?"

I climbed up to the window, stepping on the bricks that made up her home and stuck my head into the window putting my face near hers. "Meet us at our spot when you can. These three *imbéciles*have something to tell you."

Clarisse bit her lip and nodded. "Give me half an hour." She looked into the other room. 'I will have to escape Mother." She explained.

I nodded and jumped back down from the window. Val, Tomas, and I took off towards our spot, which was a small park, more like a tree and some grass really, near my house. It was in the middle of a small neighborhood and most of the time the tree was full of lush green leaves. The grass had that nice fresh smell. Dandelions spotted the grass like freckles on skin and the tree was a big oak, probably older than my father and maybe even his father. Val, Tomas, and I sat around the tree each of our backs to it, leaning against it in a circle. It was how we did it, in case someone had troubling news or an embarrassing story, we did not have to see the faces of the other people. The old tree had probably heard more secrets and stories than any other. Soon enough Clarisse came and sat down next to Val and me, her face flushed from rushing. Once they all sat, I told them my tale.

"I heard from my uncle, and you cannot share this with anyone, please. I was not even supposed to hear this, but my uncle has reason to believe that Gustave Eiffel is going to get assassinated."

Three other voices filled my ears, all of them asking questions at once.

"One at a time, one at a time!" I yelled, turning back and looking at them in frustration. They quieted down and I continued. "I do not have much information right now but I'm going to look into it."

"But Al, there have been rumors like this going on for ages. Why do you think this one is true?" Tomas asked, voicing his concern.

"I know Tomas, which is why I wanted to see what other information my uncle knows," I explained.

"Isn't your uncle coming to help on the project of the Tower? Is that how he got the information?" Clarisse asked.

I nodded then remembered that they could not see me. "Yes, I believe so." I got up and dusted myself off from the grass and faced my friends. "I'm going to need some help later on, but I'm thinking that this one is a real threat. My uncle seemed so sure of it."

Clarisse and the others got up as well, dusting off their own clothes. Clarisse looked concerned. "Al, this could be nothing more than a rumor," She cautioned.

Val and Tomas nodded in agreement. "We will believe you when you have some proof," Tomas joked, a mischievous grin placed on his face.

I could tell my friends did not believe me, thinking it was a joke, and it made me angry, I let my voice show it as I stormed off. "Fine, I'll get some proof and then you'll all see," I shouted behind my shoulder.

"Why not go to Eiffel himself! He's at a hotel near the construction!" Val called behind me, his voice laughing. I heard Tomas laughing as well and it only made my face flush with anger and determination.

I ran all the way from the park to my apprentice shop. I was working as an apprentice for an architect, named Alexandre. He allowed me to call him "Alex". He used to be a friend of my father when my mother was alive and the three of them had been close friends. But when my mother died, eleven years ago, my father and Alex had drifted apart. They were still friendly to one another, as I was Alex's apprentice, but nothing more. The shop's bell rang as I pushed open the green door. I threw my newsboy hat onto the coat hanger and grabbed an apron from the hook and tied it around my waist. "*Monsieur* Alex, it's me, Al. I'm in for work," I called knowing that he was probably tinkering in the back with some type of part. I set myself up on the old counter upfront, helping anyone who came in asking questions. Most came to ask about the Tower, if it was possible, what types of materials were being used to build, etc. A few asked what I thought as an individual about it. I answered the best I could and soon enough there was a lull in customers, which was when Alex came out from the back. He was probably in his thirties, his large, owl-like glasses were on the bridge of his nose as he looked down at the gears in his hands. His brown hair was sticking out in every direction and his face was drawn in concentration.

"Ah, Al, so glad you're here." He looked up at me and smiled, his tan skin even darker than I last saw him, probably from too much sun. He turned the sign on the front of the door to "closed". "How do you feel about taking a trip to see the project?", He asked me, and my heart leaped in anticipation of seeing the work again.

"Absolutely!", I said, ditching the apron and grabbing my hat. Alex laughed as I shoved him through the door.

Alex acted more like an older brother than an authority figure and I applauded the man for the way he held onto the youthfulness of life. We walked at a leisurely pace through the streets before we got to the construction site. We stopped and both stared at the building. The construction had started in January of this year. Now the legs of the Tower were being added and nearly finished.

"Now what do you think of that Al?" My friend asked me as he looked at the structure.

"I should be asking you, Alex," I answered, I knew that Alex had entered into the competition that started the whole construction of the project anyway. The competition was to discover which architect could bring about a fascinating project in time for the World's Fair. Eiffel's design was the one chosen.

Alex chuckled mirthlessly. "I think the man is mad, but he has a great vision that will come to be either his greatest downfall or he will go down in history for it." He sat down on the ground, not caring if he was in the way. "Concrete, limestone, and ironwork. It will all go down when the World's Fair is over and yet many people are still worried it will even be completed. Many are out to stop the project in general," He explained.

I sat down next to him and nodded, remembering old newspapers that had headlines like: *"Gustave Eiffel has Gone Mad: Has Been Confined in an Asylum."* and *"Construction Stopped Again Completion Impossible."* I picked up some of the grass that was scattered around and pulled the blades apart. "Alex," I started, "Do you think someone might want to get rid of Gustave Eiffel?" I looked over at him and he pursed his lips in thought.

"I do not know Al, there are lots of people opposed to the whole thing. Yes, there have been some rumors going around about Eiffel going to be hurt or assassinated but I do not know if anyone would be crazy enough to go through with it. *Mon Dieu*, could you imagine that." He laughed and I relaxed a little, my shoulders falling from where they had hitched up from anticipation and tension.

I nodded. What Alex said made sense, but I could not be sure until I talked to my uncle or father. I had to know. I *had* to. If it were true would I condemn an innocent man to death because I did not do anything to stop it?

***

When I got home that evening, I was exhausted but eager to start my investigation. My father was home and, in his study, and I knocked to let him know I was there. My father looked over at me and smiled, waving me in. "How was your day Al?" He asked me.

I nodded, "It was fine Father, but I have a question." I said, leaning against his desk. "Do you think something will happen to Gustave Eiffel?"

My father stared at the paper in hand for a moment before sighing deeply and looking up at me. "Aleron, answer me right now. Did you overhear your uncle and I talking about anything?" His voice was stern and his face even more so.

I quickly backpedaled. My intentions of getting found out were in the furthest reaches of my mind. "No!" I lied, something that was easy for me to do, especially after my mother died. It was easy to lie and say I was fine, or school was good, or that the fight was my fault than to worry my father more. He had enough to handle already without my problems adding on. I shook my head. "No, I did not. I was simply curious. Rumors are going around, you know, and Alex was talking about it." I knew that the best way to lie was to add little bits of truth to it.

My Father studied me before nodding. "No, I do not think anything will happen to Gustave Eiffel. Those rumors are just that, rumors." He turned back to his papers and I knew I was dismissed.

"Yes, Father," I said and walked out of the study.

I set about making dinner, wondering when my uncle was going to come home from his meetings with the other architects, mathematicians, and those who were part of Gustave Eiffel's team on the Tower. Dinner passed with just my father and I. An awkward silence that had not been a part of the meal in such a long time, was there that night, something that hadn't been missed. I wanted it gone but did not know how to get rid of it. Afterward, I went to my room, grabbing a random book and opening it I started reading just to pass the time. I had a plan in my head, but everyone had to be asleep for me to even try it. My uncle got home late that evening, and the sun had already set. I listened to my father's voice greeting him. I heard them say good night and I sat in my room for another hour just to be sure. I grabbed an oil lamp and lit it, taking off my shoes but leaving my sock on so I could slide around the wood floors. I held the lamp in front of me and walked to my uncle's room. The door was closed so I opened it. I was not aware of how loud things became at night until that very moment. The door creaked and I held my breath. My uncle stayed asleep, his snores deafening for anything coming near three feet of him. I walked to the small table that was on the side of the room, the floorboards creaking, with every step. Adrenaline was coursing through my veins, making me sweat, and I knew that I had to get this done quickly. I opened the table drawer, the pieces of wood scraping against each other. I winced and bit my bottom lip to keep myself from making sounds. I pulled out my uncle's satchel, the one he always carried. The old leather was soft and the papers inside crinkled from being moved. I unbuckled the two gold buckles and flipped it open carefully. I placed the lamp on the floor and pulled out all the papers. Most were just sketches, drawings of projects, and math equations that I could not even understand. I found travel papers and train tickets.

"Useless, useless. Come on, there must be something," I whispered to myself, growing impatient. I put all of the papers back the right way and was just about to give up when something slipped out, fluttering to the ground. I snatched it up. The paper was a telegram. I brought it close to the lamp and turned up the flame. I looked at the paper and tried to read it. The block lettering that was typed out read:Gustave Eiffel in danger. stop. be assassinated if not stopped. stop. tell no one. stop. You are warned. stop. it will happen before the World Fair. stop. Do not repeat. I stared at the telegram, reading it twice. There was no name given for the sender. I copied the information on another piece of paper, taking some charcoal and writing it out. My uncle shifted in his bed and my heart rate spiked. I grabbed all of his stuff and put it back in the satchel, including the

20

telegram and booked it out of his room as quietly as I could. I sat down on my own bed a few minutes later staring at the words. How did my uncle get this? There was no return sender and no name. Why did he have it? And who sent it? This piece of information, no matter how small it was, seemed to have opened a bigger box of questions. I thought for a moment before I had an answer. I knew where to go, and who to question. It would have to be to the man himself, Gustave Eiffel. I was coming for him and my only hope was that I could save him in time.

Chapter Three - La Confrontation de Gustave Eiffel

*The confrontation of Gustave Eiffel...*what was I doing, what was I thinking?! Me, a kid, one that my own father barely took seriously, was going to talk to Eiffel? I had to find a way to do it. I had to find answers even to just appease my own mind. The next morning, I skipped school and evaded my father's questions. I held onto my copied version of the telegram and headed to the telegram office. After some careful questions with the message boy and his boss, I got nowhere in the investigation, other than the fact that they had not seen anyone come in the past couple of weeks that needed to send or pick up a telegram. It was another dead end. I was struggling with my inner will as to whether I should continue chasing rumors, but every time I thought I should just stop and crumble up that telegram I couldn't not think about the fact that it might be true.

After much contemplation, I decided what I should do. I headed to the hotel where basically everyone knew where Eiffel was staying, the news was made public thanks to the newspapers that would declare amazement one week then criticize the next. I hurried across town, passing busy shops, bakeries that I had to force myself past, and finally made it to his hotel. I held out the telegram and showed the back of it to the front desk. "Telegram for *Monsieur* Gustave Eiffel," I said, pulling my newsboy hat a little over my face. The clerk gave me his hotel room number and I also asked them for a few pieces of paper and a writing utensil. Without hesitation, I shot up the stairs that were heading to the next levels. I climbed them, skipping steps with my long legs. At nearly six feet my height had its advantages. I shoved the telegram into my pocket as I found his room number. I took in a deep breath and knocked on the door. A butler was quick to answer, which surprised me, and I took a hesitant step backward.

"I was wondering if I could talk to *Monsieur* Eiffel?" I asked. The demand that I was aiming for came out as more of a question.

The butler stared at me for a moment before turning around and calling into the room. "Gustave, there is a boy here saying he wishes to speak to you." He turned back to me, his dark eyes filled with disdain and his mustache twitched.

I heard footsteps before I looked into the room and saw the very man himself, looking alive and well. His black and grey hair was curly and swept up, slick looking. His long Roman nose was accurately fitted for his face and his round face completed the look of a smart man at ease in his surroundings. He greeted me with a smile, and for some reason, I gave a small one back almost on instinct.

"Maurice, let the boy in, I am sure it is nothing." Gustave waved me in, and I gave a hesitant step around the man that was in the doorway, his eyes calculating as he watched me move. I realized that this was not a butler as I first had thought, but was, in fact, a friend of Eiffel's.

Gustave turned his attention back to Maurice, who was the man at the door and waved him off. "Go home Maurice, it was lovely seeing you, my friend."

Maurice nodded, which was his goodbye and he left, closing the door behind him. Gustave turned to me and I stared into his sharp gaze. "So, what brings a young lad like you to my door?" He asked, waving me into the sitting room of his hotel suite.

I cleaned my throat, suddenly nervous, and wiped my free hand on my pants. "Well, sir, *Monsieur*... I was hoping to ask you some questions," I started.

Eiffel took a seat in one of the sitting chairs, crossing his legs as he sat and eased back into the chair almost like my presence did not bother him. "Oh, what kind of questions, lad? Something for the paper? For your own personal interest, or for your father perhaps?" He asked, raising a slightly bushy eyebrow at me in question.

"I-well, to be honest- I, I," I said so eloquently, wanting to slap my hand across my forehead to get my brain working. I took in a calming breath and tried a different approach. "Do you often let strangers into your hotel rooms?", I questioned him, furrowing my brows and tilting my head.

Gustave laughed, the sound rich and unexpected. "I like you, boy. Come ask your questions." He chuckled, sipping from a cup of tea that suddenly appeared in his hand as I did not see him make it, but he could have possibly had it on the table already and I missed it. I was not really thinking straight at this point.

I moved to sit on one of the chairs and carefully pulled the telegram out of my pocket. "I wanted to ask your opinion on this."

I handed it to him, and he took it with a sudden seriousness that had not come from the man yet.

"Where did you get this?" He asked, his voice thoughtful as he read the typed-out words.

"From a friend." I lied, using his confusion to my advantage. "I want to know if you think it could be true."

He handed it back to me, his eyes looking intently on the paper as I folded it and put it in my pocket. "I think anything could be true," He replied.

I looked at him, slight confusion, mixed with awe on my face. "Does it not concern you that you just read something like that? I mean your life could very well hang in the balance over this project."

Gustave suddenly stood up, putting down his tea and went to go stand by the window, with a view clear enough that he could see the construction on said project. He stared out the window for a moment. I wondered if he was scared at all, then he turned back to me. "What was your name again?"

"Aleron. Aleron Arago," I supplied, watching the man as he walked around his room, a hand on his chin in thought.

"Arago...that sounds familiar," He said, coming to stop behind his chair, resting his hands on the back of it.

I struggled to follow where he was going with this but answered all the same. "My uncle, he's working with you on the Tower. François Arago," I offered.

Eiffel nodded, "Ah, that is where it's from." He paused. "Now to answer your question. Let me say this first. What do *you* think of the project?", He asked genuinely.

I thought about it for a moment then answered honestly. "I think it's amazing, and it's something that I look forward to seeing being built. It's an architect's dream."

The man nodded, seemingly pleased with the answer. "Good. There are...others out there that do not want to see my project completed." He went to stare out the window for a moment and I saw that he was remembering something. He seemed to shake himself out of it and smiled back at me. "If there is anyone who wants to see me dead it would probably be *Le Comité de Trois Cents.*"

At my confused face, he continued. "The Committee of Three Hundred they call themselves, a person for each meter my tower is high," Eiffel explained. He moved over to a dark wood desk in the corner of the room and pulled out a few pieces of paper from the drawer. "They've called it The Vulgar Tower, my beautiful project and they're ashamed to have it in the city," He said, handing me the papers. "I looked into it and personally wrote down the name of each person against me." He chuckled, sitting back down. "I planned on writing them a letter proclaiming how wrong they each were when the Tower was finished. A little gloating but what man isn't proud of what he accomplishes."

I took the pages, looking at them like they were the answer to all of the universe's problems. They were not, obviously, but I was still amazed that I now had a firm grasp of this world. My investigation finally had a lead. "Why are you giving this to me?" I asked, wondering as to why he was being so nice.

"Because...you asked questions," Gustave gave as an answer. He smiled and I knew that he was hiding something in that smile, something that I desperately wanted to know. He pointed at the paper, giving me a few names. "The Committee is being led by the prominent architect Charles Garnier. I would ask him some of your important questions. The man has always been against me, ever since I won the contest of the century and he did not."

Monsieur Eiffel told me a little bit more about the Committee, how it was composed of artists, writers, painters, sculptors, and architects. There was an article published in the newspaper *Le Temps* earlier in the year about the tower and Eiffel showed me the clipping he saved from the paper. The article completely decimated the tower, and the creator Eiffel himself, calling the tower a *"ridiculous tower dominating Paris like a gigantic black smokestack."*

He told me how he felt he was proud of his tower, how it was a truly eventful creation that he longed to bring to reality. I realized that as he was telling me all of this, that the man had to believe that some of the rumors, the accusations, the threats, were somewhat true because he was worried. Gustave handed me the papers with the names again. "I do not know if it will help you find your answers for your 'friend'," He said, raising an eyebrow with the hint of a smile on his face. "But, if it's any help, you should start looking there."

"Are you not worried that something might happen just like the telegram said?" I asked. "It says before the World's Fair, that's only a few months from now." I asked, throwing up my hands a little in exasperation.

Eiffel stood up and clasped my shoulder. "My boy, I will not worry about that as I've only been meant to be in this world for a little while. With days that pass quicker than a painter's stroke on a canvas I can only hope to leave my mark with my projects." He squeezed my shoulder. "My tower will be completed. It will be finished. My tower will be the tallest

27

edifice ever erected by man. Will it not also be grandiose in its own way?"

I nodded, too overwhelmed with different emotions to speak. I took my papers and stood. "*Merci, Monsieur.*" I shook Gustave Eiffel's hand and opened his hotel door. Before he closed it, I turned back again. "Why are you helping me?" I asked one more time, hoping for a better answer.

Gustave gave me that secret smile again, one that hid behind facades and whit. "Because Aleron, you asked questions." He gave the answer to me with a nod, then closed the door. Our conversation was seemingly over.

I looked down at the wonderful papers I had in my hand. I finally had a lead! The only problem now was that my lead was three *hundred* people long. I did not know where to start.

Chapter Four - Montrer Et Dire

Show and tell, that is what it felt like that next day when I called my friend back to our spot with actual proof in my hands. I was not one to just go and do something without actual facts and knowledge but now that I had the chance to meet

Gustave himself, it gave me much to think about. Our friendship, the four of us, Val, Tomas, Clarisse, and I, was an odd one. In a time where most men and women were segregated, we'd actually grown closer to each other as we grew up. I considered them my best friends. It was difficult, as life continued, as responsibilities piled up, and, at least for Clarisse, suitors started coming in. We were seeing each other whenever we could because if life has taught me anything from the loss of my mother, it was that people are not meant to stay for a long time. So, cherish each moment you have with them. Memories are over like a flip of a coin and when it falls to the ground you are wondering if you are heads or tails, spinning in confusion over the loss of a friend or a loved one. I walked with meaningful steps, full of purpose until I got to the first of my friends' houses.

I knocked on the door and Tomas' little sister opened the door. Her brown soulful eyes were big as she looked up at me.

"Hi," I said, waving my hand, wondering which of Tomas' little sisters this was. "Is Tomas here? It's his friend Al," I offered. (Getting slightly creeped out as she kept staring at me.)

She did not say anything but instead took in a deep breath and yelled for her brother. I cringed at the volume of her scream and was glad to hear footsteps.

"Marie! Shut up, would you? *Mon Dieu.*" Tomas sighed, opening the door more as she took off inside the house, her mission completed. "Go help *mère.*" He called, even though Marie was more than halfway gone. Tomas sighed heavily before he turned to me.

"What is it, Al?", He questioned, looking unconcerned.

"Can you meet again at our spot?", I implored him, hope flooding my system.

Tomas nodded but slumped against the doorframe. "Why?" He asked, a groan in his voice.

"If you come then I'll tell you." I added. "But you have to come."

Tomas growled. "You're a pain in my rear Aleron. You really are."

I stuck my tongue out at him and left. I collected Val and we both made our way towards Clarisse's house. We stopped short when we saw her talking to a young man we had never seen before. She was talking but as soon as she saw us, she stopped and bid the man a good day. The man looked at me for a moment, and he tipped his hat at Clarisse before leaving. He was a little older than us, perhaps early twenties.

"Who was that?" I demanded, pointing to the man's retreating back.

"Just a suitor, nothing to worry about," Clarisse said, fixing her bonnet straps.

"How come we have never seen him before?" Val questioned, taking the words out of my mouth.

Clarisse sighed, exasperated. "He lives outside of Paris," She explained. "Now what do you need me for?"

I could not stop the flare of jealousy I felt at seeing Clarisse meeting another man. I shook it off and answered her question. "I want to meet at our spot. I have some particularly important news." I pulled out my papers from my pant pocket and waved them in front of her. "I have proof."

Val scoffed behind me. "Sure, you do Al, sure you do."

I whacked him over the head with the papers, making a satisfying noise. "Just you wait, *vous fauteur de troubles.*"

Val shoved my shoulder, "I'm not a troublemaker, you are! Just think about your father right now."

I winced and bit my lip. If my father knew what I was doing, he would have tanned my hide before I could even get a word out. We walked to our spot, Val joining us later, just in time for me to tell them what I had found. For once I made them all face me, as I said, "Okay, you guys will not believe what I found."

Clarisse raised an eyebrow but that was the only acknowledgment that I got from the three of them.

"Are you going to tell us what you found, or are you going to stand there shaking in excitement like a little dog?" Tomas pointed out, a smirk forming on his lips.

I considered smacking him like I did Val with the papers in my hand but instead, I took a deep breath and showed them the paper Eiffel gave me. *"Le Comité de Trois Cents."*

"The Committee of Three hundred? What does that have to do with anything?" Clarisse asked, a frown on her face.

I sat down on the grass, some of the sharp blades poking through the fabric of my pants. "The Committee is my suspect pool. If I need to figure out who might kill Eiffel I need to start there. I went to the man himself, Gustave Eiffel, and got these papers from him."

A sharp laugh came from Val. "You! You expect us to believe you met Eiffel himself, and they just let you up and he told you all his secrets." He laughed again, "That is rich Al."

I shrugged and nodded. "That is pretty much what happened." I had lied a little to get what I wanted but essentially that is what happened. "Eiffel himself told me about the Committee, who it was run by, even the names of each person in the group."

Clarisse gently put a hand on my knee. "Aleron, that's all public knowledge. He could be just leading you on a simple goose chase. Something to make him laugh."

I thought about the way Gustave acted, how he seemed genuinely concerned. I'd barely talked with the man for more than half an hour, but he seemed like a good man. I shook my head. "No, I do not think that is it." I shifted the papers out on the lawn, showing the names and information to my friends. "The Committee is being run by a man named Charles Garnier, who Eiffel says hates him. If we can divide it by four, which gives us seventy-five people each we can interview almost every day after school and..."

"Whoa, whoa, wait a minute," Tomas said, crossing his arms. "Who said we are going to help you?"

My mouth froze as did my thoughts. "What?" I squeaked out. "Of course, you're going to help me, right?" My heart sank into my stomach when Val and Tomas got up at once.

Val looked sadder than Tomas did for leaving, but both had definite defiance in their eyes. "I'm sorry Al, I have an actual job to do. I do not have time for rumors and fake news."

Tomas nodded, dusting off his pants. "Al, this is beyond stupid to put time and energy into this. It all could be fake. Why are you deciding to investigate this one thread of possibility when numerous amounts of the same rumors are floating around. None have become true and you know it."

I stood up angrily, my eyes narrowing as I looked at them. "And if it is true? Isn't it our duty as the people of France to keep our city safe?! What happens if I did happen to choose the one thread of truth that was actually viable, then we would be saving a man! An innocent man!" I was yelling by the time I finished speaking.

Tomas met my challenge and pointed a finger in my face. "You do not know if he's innocent! What if he is not Al!? Then what?" He yelled at me, his fingers curling into fists.

"Then we still would have been saving someone's life." I answered, getting ready to be on the defense as I watched my friend's fists.

Val suddenly got in the middle of us, forcing us apart. "Stop it! Both of you," He commanded.

Tomas and I's chests were heaving from angry breaths as I stared him down.

"I am not the one looking for something for my father to be proud of," Tomas sneered. "Aleron is the one longing to be loved. Well I'm sure going after a stupid rumor will definitely get his attention."

I pushed against Val's arms holding me back. "What did you say?" I growled, my feet digging into the ground as Val fought to keep me away.

Tomas continued taunting. "At least I have a parent who loves me, I am sure your mother is wondering why she had such a *stupid* son. One dumb enough to go after lies."

When Tomas mentioned my mother, I saw red. I pushed myself away from Val roughly and marched to Tomas, punching him square in the jaw. "How dare you talk about my mother!", I snapped. Tomas' hat flew off from the force of my punch and he sneered at me and tackled me to the ground.

I heard Clarisse scream, but I was too busy trying to block the force of Tomas's attack. We wrestled in the grass, with dirt and grass blades flying this way and that. I ended up on top and punched him straight in the face, hearing his nose crack. I was so involved in my fury I did not feel Val pull me away from Tomas, shouts of my name coming from both Clarisse and Val's lips. I fought, but eventually let him pull me away.

Tomas got up to his elbows, a hand covering his face as blood ran from his nose. "*Mon Dieu*! You're an animal!" He spit blood into the grass and got up. Clarisse came over to steady him. "You're crazy!", He fumed.

"Ta gueule!" I shouted, daring him to speak again. I struggled against Val who had a death grip against my stomach. "How dare you speak about my mother!"

Tomas cursed at me, shook off Clarisse's hand and left, holding a hand to his shining red nose. Val released me and shook his head at me.

"What are you doing Al?!", He barked at me. "Huh?! What was that?", Val asked, waving a hand towards Tomas's leaving form. "You can do this whole thing yourself," He decided, grabbing his jacket that he bought and put it on.

Clarisse looked at me, her eyes wide with shock and fear, but her bottom lip trembled as if she wanted to cry. "Let it go Al," She whispered, before grabbing her skirt and running off after Val, her breath catching in a way I knew she was going to cry.

I watched my friends walk away, each one of their reactions striking my chest like knives to my heart. I swallowed thickly.

"I am not crazy," I said to myself. I clenched my jaw in anger, otherwise tears would have been streaming down my face. I picked up the thrown papers from the ground, dusting off the dirt from them and smoothing them out. "And I am not letting it go."

I watched them a little longer, seeing Clarisse as the only one who looked back at me. Her eyes still held fear, but now there was pity, something that I did not want thrown at me. I tucked my papers under my arm and left, the words of hurt that my friends had said replaying in my mind. I never should have brought them into this. I should have kept it to myself. Right then and there I decided that I was going to solve it, just me. I made a dismissive noise in the back of my throat.

"Forget them then," I said only to myself. Hesitating, I looked back just once, and they were gone. It was almost as if they had not been there at all. "I can do this myself," I promised.

I took off at a run. I had someone to talk to: Charles Garnier. My resolve was strengthened by my anger and by my hurt from my friends. I ran until I was home, slamming the door shut and I made it to my room. I took a few deep breaths to keep the painful emotions at bay. I could not believe that my own friends did not believe me. If they did not, how was I going to make any stranger believe me if I found any evidence that actually *was* true. I sat on the floor and leaned back against my bed, putting my face in my hands.

Later on, I do not know how much later, I heard a knocking on my front door. Whoever it was, they were persistent as the knocking got louder. My uncle and father were in our parlor, not to be disturbed, so I rushed as fast as I could, muttering apologies along the way as I opened the door.

I froze when I saw Clarisse there. I knew it was after her curfew and she was wearing...pants?

"What are you doing here?", I wanted to know, coming outside and closing the door to the house. "And what are you wearing?"

Clarisse sighed, "They are just pants, same as you. I took my father's and sewed my own pair. They are much easier to travel in, and many ladies in Paris are wearing them."

I blinked at her.

"Right, you're not looking for the latest fashions. *Excusez-moi.*" She sighed again, resigned, and looked up at me with her piercing blue eyes. "I came to help. I want in."

"What?!" I asked, shocked, as my eyes grew wide. Clarisse seemed to read through me with her gaze and I swallowed. "Why?" I questioned, turning skeptical.

Clarisse took a step closer to me. I heard her breathing. We were so close now. "I care for you Al," the words stilling the blood in my veins. "I want to help. I...I do not know if these rumors are true, but, if they are, and I do not help you in some way, in any way, I will feel that in my heart forever," She explained. Her eyes were dark with regret but light with hope at the same time.

I thought about it before nodding once. "Okay," I relented. My heart leapt when she laughed joyfully and kissed me on the cheek. I stared, stunned at her, as she stepped away again, her lips burning a memory into my face.

"What is your next step?", She petitioned, a smile on her face. "You do have a plan do you not?"

A nervous laugh escaped me. "I do, kind of." I cleared my throat, feeling a blush travel over my face and neck. "In the morning we can talk to Charles Garnier. We can figure out where he lives and ask him some questions. From there I do not know."

Clarisse nodded solemnly. "It's a start, and that is better than what you had earlier."

I mentally agreed. "You should probably go home now, it's late. I do not want you getting in trouble." That was truthfully the furthest thing from my mind at the moment. I did not want her getting hurt at all. Period. If I brought her into this, I was taking the risk that she would remain safe.

Clarisse and I wished each other good night and I waited until she was out of sight before coming back into the house.

I slid down the door and slumped onto the floor. "What did I just do?" I asked myself. I laughed; a tad bit hysterical if I was being truthful. The only help I was going to be getting was from the girl that I had had a crush on since I was little more than a boy. How was I going to do this? I shook my head before standing up and heading back into my bedroom. I was in trouble now. I shook my head. "*Quelle pagaille!*", I breathed out, exasperated. What a mess! I fell asleep that night hoping beyond hope that I had not made the wrong decision by accepting Clarisse's offer of help.

Chapter Five - La Lettre Disait

The letter said to stop, that I was warned. I should have taken that warning seriously. The events that transpired were the beginning of the end. Let us continue, as the story goes... so do the consequences.

The following morning when Clarisse knocked on my door, I skipped school. This was not an easy feat, but I had learned to master it by now. I avoided Tomas and Val, coming up on Clarisse's house to knock on her door.

Her father answered, a stern man in his late forties. He had the same eyes as his daughter but there was more anger in them. His graying hair made him look distinguished and all the more intimidating. I knew that Clarisse's family was well to do as her father owned some type of shipping business for France. What I knew was that I was too poor to make it onto the suitor's list that her family had for her, but still, I could hope. I would be marrying outside of my station, but I didn't let it deter me from liking Clarisse. She was a treasure any man could want. I thought I was lucky enough just to be her friend. For her to stick by my side through this meant everything. Her kiss on my cheek still burned in my memory.

"*Bonjour Monsieur,*" I started. "I was hoping to see Clarisse."

The door was slammed in my face. I stood there blinking at it for half a minute before it opened again. Clarisse stood there when it reopened

"I'm so sorry about that. My father can be a little overprotective sometimes," She said, almost shyly.

I smiled to put her at ease. "No worries." I shook the address I had in my hand. "Are you ready to talk to Charles Garnier?"

She smiled, eyes shining like crystals, as she nodded in excitement. "Where does he live?"

I had retrieved the address from the post office, which was where I got the information from my uncle's telegram. "He lives in the outskirts of Paris. We will need to take a carriage or something-"

"Ooh, we can take your bike!", Clarisse examined. "I just need to change into my pants, so give me a second. *Merci.*"

I watched her turn back into the house, and she was gone before I could even get another word out. She came out in record time, with brown pants on and determination filling every part of her. Clarisse was fixing her tan shirt, tucking it in when she reached me again.

"Let us head over," I said, gesturing for her to follow me. "*Allons-y!*"

We walked step in step for a while, with a gust of wind blowing Clarisse's hair about. She tried to blow it out of her face and undo the tangles but to no avail. Even with her hair becoming a rat's nest, and dressed in men's clothes, she was still beautiful.

We were nearing my house, which was a block or two from hers. The silence between us was surprisingly comfortable, considering yesterday's events when Clarisse suddenly threw up her hands and growled, "I wish I had brought a ribbon or something! This blasted hair always gets in my way." She sighed, "I should have brought my bonnet." Her features pinched and she gathered her hair to the back of her neck and simply held it back with her hand. She looked over at me and glanced at my head. "You are lucky you are a boy Al. You do not have to worry about things like this. No suitors, no hair troubles, no dresses, and you get to finish schooling..." She faded off.

I nodded. I *was* thankful I was a boy when she listed things like that. Being a boy had its own challenges, but I kept my inquiries to myself. I opened my mouth to speak when I remembered something. "Clarisse, here," I reached into my pocket and felt around a bit. When the cool piece of colored silk touched my fingers, I pulled it out. "You left your old one behind the last time we were all together...well some time ago, and I know you usually have your bonnet, but I saw it on the ground," My face burned as I remembered the memory. "And I, uh accidentally stepped on it. I messed it up real good, so I...got you this new one. I just remembered." I felt my face flush and I could not look as I handed it to her. It was so juvenile to think she would accept it, I had kept it in my pocket until I had the right moment togive it to her. I had saved up and bought it from the mercantile. Our fingers brushed as she took it from me, and I could not help but glance back at her face. She was smiling as bright as the afternoon sun. My face burned brighter. *Mon Dieu*, curse my face. I cleared my throat awkwardly and looked away from her gaze.

"Thank you, Aleron," She breathed, her eyes crinkly with joy. Clarisse gave me a look I could not understand. She quickly took her hand away and tied her hair back with the new pink ribbon. It complimented her eyes and I think she knew that. She shook her hair out a few seconds later, glad to rid it from her face. Her cheeks held a faint blush as well and I felt no small amount of pride from putting it there. We smiled at each other and I realized we made it to our destination. We had been standing still for a good five minutes.

"I will go get the bike, just wait here," I said. She nodded and I jogged off to the back of my house, picking up my bike from where it was leaning against the side of the house. As I walked it back towards her, I noticed something. We did not think this through.

The bike, obviously made for one, would not fit both of us. She had nowhere to sit.

"Clarisse!" I called as I rode it towards her, "We might have a bit of a problem." She turned at the sound of my voice and stared in puzzlement at the bike. Her brows furrowed and she glanced at the tires.

"Why? Do we have a flat?", She asked, her hands going to her hips. I shook my head as I stopped in front of her, planting one foot on a pedal and the other on the ground.

"No," I stated, "but the bike will only hold one. So how do you exactly want to do this?"

She hummed and rubbed her chin. I looked down at the bike and thought as well.

"Ah ha!," I exclaimed, and slapped the handlebars. "You can ride these," I said, a smile on my face. It was something Val, Tomas, and I did when we were younger. I ground my jaw thinking about them.

"Aleron!" She gasped, drawing my attention back towards the present, "That is indecent! And very unsafe! Do you want me to fall off and crack my head open?" She leaned towards me, her tone very cross and I realized my mistake.

I winced internally and tried to placate her. "Well no, Clarisse, I want you to be safe, but we have got to get nearly outside of Paris and we only have one bike! Do you have any better ideas?" I asked.

She smirked and crossed her arms. "In fact, I do," she stated, nodding her head once. Her smile meant trouble. Her blue eyes narrowed, and I felt my suspicion soar as she gestured for me to get off. This was not going to be good.

***

I was right. The wind rushed towards my face and made my eyes sting. I tried shifting my weight, but when the whole bike lurched, I kept still.

"Al!," Clarisse scolded from behind me, "Keep still, you will topple the bike."

"Well, excuse me!" I stated, a bit angrily, "The handlebars are pinching my behind." I could not believe she managed to rope me into this. My hands clenched the bars in a knuckle-white grip. "And you drive like a crazy person!", I exclaimed, as she nearly plowed into a tree. "Left! Take a left."

She laughed and peddled faster, "If you were a better navigator, I would steer better. You are not exactly a window, Al."

I huffed and tried to ignore the looks we received when we rushed by pedestrians. A teenage boy on the handlebars of *his* bike while a young girl peddled and steered for them. Ridiculous. I shook my head and sighed as much as I could without having a panic attack as we crossed a busy street. I whipped back at her to glare and meet her cheeky smile. Girls are crazy. Clarisse in particular.

We managed to get to Charles Garnier's house without incident. We had a few near-death experiences, but nothing that would cause a delay. The house was quaint but elegant in its design. I could tell it was the house of an architect. With a questioning glance at Clarisse, we went ahead and walked up the drive to the large iron door. I knocked loudly, the sound echoing. It took a moment before someone answered the door. A man, who I guessed to be Garnier, stood in front of us. His face reminded me of a hound, somewhat long and droopy, and his head was very flat on top. He looked to be in his sixties, brown hair, mostly grey. He was wearing a suit worn mostly by the richer men that were in Clarisse's neighborhood.

"Charles Garnier?" I asked.

The man nodded his head, tilting it to the side as he looked at me. "Yes?" He had a thicker French accent than most.

Giving a quick look to Clarisse to follow my lead, I let the lies fall from my lips. I introduced myself and then Clarisse. "Good evening Sir, I am writing a paper for my school, the newspaper you see. I was hoping to get your opinion on the project Gustave Eiffel is conducting."

Charles looked at me for one calculating moment, before he stepped back and opened the door more. "Come in, we can talk in my study."

I was amazed at how easily people take others' words for the truth. Twice now I had managed to simply walk in to talk to two major suspects in my Eiffel investigation, amazed that people could believe you are trustworthy until given a reason to think otherwise.

He led up to a large dark room, masculine in design, and had many rich colors like dark purple, brown, and black. He motioned for both of us to sit in the chairs that occupied the room. His chair, or at least the one he sat in, was by a brick fireplace, unlit of course, as it was the warmer months of the year. Clarisse and I sat side by side, each of us at appropriate lengths away from each other. "What is your newspaper called, *les jeunes*?"

Before I could even think of a name, Clarisse smiled and joined the hoax.

"*L'inquisition*. The whole school works on it for a small paper we print." Her innocent smile sold the words that she spoke. The inquisition was not a bad name for a fake paper.

Charles ran a bell suddenly. A maid came in, bowed a little at the waist, and waited for her order. "Please bring in some tea for me and my young guests," He ordered, and she scurried off again. "What are your concerns about Gustave Eiffel and his project?"

I shifted in the seat. I was fully aware of my slightly dirty trousers on the clean chair. "Well *Monsieur*, we received word that you are the leader of the *Le Comité de Trois Cents.* We would like to know why you are so opposed to Eiffel's tower."

"We would also like to address the rumors that have been circulating throughout Paris about someone out to assassinate Eiffel. Do you think those hold any merit?" Clarisse added, a bit to the point, I liked her bluntness. She still looked at home in the fancy setting, even with her own pair of pants and her slightly messy hair. I wished I had the same comfortable feeling. I had come here almost without any sort of plan and I felt lost in a situation where I needed full control. I could not fully get a reading on Garnier, as I could with Eiffel, and it bothered me.

"*Le Comité de Trois Cents,* is something that was needed," Charles started, pausing to accept the tray of tea that the maid had brought, he offered some to both Clarisse and I, but I did not feel like tea at the moment. He stirred a small spoon into the cup as he thought about what to say, I noticed that he did not take any sugar. Something about the way he stirred his spoon and stared at me reminded me in a way of my mother, her stern gaze only used with me when I was in trouble.

"Gustave and I met when we both entered into the World's Fair's competition of 1886, to create something so illustrious that it would be the centerpiece of attraction for the people who came to the fair. Obviously, as you know, Gustave won. With his plans of a three-hundred-meter-high tower." He said this almost like he was repeating it to us from a written statement. His face held no emotions. He was simply stating facts. Charles took a sip of his tea, before continuing. "Here is something for your paper. Tell the others here is what I think about Gustave's tower. It is nothing other than an ill-reputed interpretation of Egypt's pyramids. Has he no original thoughts? Does he need to borrow something from an ancient civilization, instead of something of his own design?"

45

The veracity of his words surprised me. There was a slightly hidden animosity in Garnier's words. Before we could say or ask another question to Charles, he put his tea down and stood up abruptly, pacing to the side of the room and back as he got riled up.

"I was an apprentice to Louis-Hippolyte Lebas," He paused and turned around to the both of us again. "Do you children know who that is?"

Neither of us did know so we shook our heads, left to right.

Charles scoffed and waved his hand to the side like he was sweeping the whole idea out of the air. "Of course, you do not! He was a French architect that had a Neoclassical style, not yet emboldened by my visions. I was a student at *École Royale des Beaux-Arts de Paris*. I obtained an estimated French scholarship at age twenty-three. I was not much older than you and I had already done much more with my life."

I bristled at this comment, I could tell Garnier was a man full of himself and his accomplishments.

He continued, pacing all the while. "I have won many competitions. In fact, Napoleon III chose my work, and it led to the magnificent opera house, *Palais Garneier*, named after myself, of course."

I noticed that there seemed to be a running theme with great architects.

"The opera house was finished in January of 1875. Many of the most prestigious monarchs of Europe attended my opening ceremony, including Marshal MacMahon, the president of France, mind you. The Lord Mayor of London, and even the bloody king of Spain! And yet, here in my own city, I failed to win against the second rate, half-wit, Gustave Eiffel. I created the Committee to take his head out of the clouds for a while, showing him the reality of what real work required." He smirked, his mustache twitching as it slowly turned into a grin.

"As for the fact that there are people braver than me out to get him, well, I applaud them. If any are lucky to succeed, then I shall indeed be ever in their debt." He sat back down and picked up his tea again. His monologue was apparently over.

I felt incredibly hot under my collar, clenching my teeth to avoid saying anything disrespectful to the man in front of me. "Do you think anyone in your Committee might actually do something dangerous?"

Charles nodded. "There are several advocates that are willing to take him down. Their names however I have conveniently forgotten." He smiled again, this time with malice and I stood up angrily.

"I have never met a more stuck up, full of himself, distasteful, *jealous* man!" My manners that my father had spent so much time drilling into my head left without so much as a goodbye as I yelled at Garnier.

Clarisse gasped at my outburst. "Aleron!"

I ignored her. "How dare you consume a man to threats of death over a competition! Are you not supposed to be the adult here, because all I see before me is a childish act of jealousy."

My head whipped to the side from the swift slap, the common way to handle a disrespectful child. My face stung as Charles Garner stood in front of me, hand still raised from where it had come across my cheek.

"Hold your tongue boy. When you are *actually* an adult you will leave these situations to those who have authority. Gustave Eiffel is none of your concern, so stop trying to pry into things that are no more than rumors." He glared at me, but I refused to back down.

"If you know, tell us." My cheek ached from where he had hit me, but I would not show that it bothered me in front of him. "Do you know anyone who would be willing to hurt Eiffel?"

Garnier took a step back from me, sitting back in his chair. "Look around you boy, the whole of Paris is out to get the man. If I knew who it was I would not be talking to an imbecilic boy who thinks he knows Eiffel better than I do, the man and his tower can go die in a ditch for all I care. Now, if you do not mind, leave my home."

I sneered at him, taking a step forward when Clarisse grabbed my arm. "Come on Al, he does not know." Her firm grip on my arm led me out of the house, my fury boiling near the surface. I yanked myself from her grasp the moment we were out of the house.

"Aleron Aragon! What were you thinking?" She yelled at me.

I spun around and pointed at that house, towering over Clarisse slightly. "That man knows nothing helpful, he is just a jealous old pig and does not care if Eiffel lives or dies!" My hopes and expectations of Garnier helping us were shattered and I felt the heavy weight of anxiety and despair try to swallow me. "He was supposed to help us Clarisse! Not give us more dead ends," I growled in frustration, running my hands through my hair, making it go crazy. It had already been two weeks since the whole thing started. Time was going so much faster than I was, and the World's Fair was arriving in less than a month and a half. I still did not know *anything* more than a couple of speculations and rumors. I felt so riled up I knew I needed to clear my head before I said or did something I regretted.

"Go ahead and ride back home. I'm going to walk," I told Clarisse, giving her the bike and waited until she climbed on.

"Al, are you sure? It's a long walk. You'll make it home by nighttime." She tried joking. "I can sit on the handlebars this time."

I gave her a small smile, a barely-there quirk of my lips. "I'm fine Clarisse, just go before you get in trouble. I need to think." I started walking beside her as she slowly started to pedal. "Besides, my father is working with my uncle on some project of his tonight, so they won't be back till late. I'll sneak in my window if I have to."

She gave me a sad look before stopping the bike and quickly kissing my cheek again. "I think what you are doing is very brave." Clarisse then got back on the bike and peddled off, leaving me to watch her retreating back, with a hand against my cheek.

     I walked for what seemed like days, so lost in thought. It really wasn't days, only an hour, possibly two, by the time I reached my neighborhood's outskirts. The day had turned into dusk, and the buildings creating beautiful shadows against the darkening orange and yellow of the setting sun. A cool breeze released some of the tension in my shoulders as I inhaled the scents that surrounded me. The bakery on Pierre Street made fresh bread, raisin pastries, and fluffy madeleines. My favorite pastry when I could afford to get one. My mother, Amelia, would wake up early and bake when my father had a rough day at the school or when I was not feeling good. I missed those days when life was a lot simpler. My mother is someone I thought about often. I almost never called her by name because of the order my father gave me when I was six, an order that I have not broken. My mother once told me that her nickname, the one my father called her, Ami, meant "dearly loved". I knew that was true when my father told me not to speak my mother's name anymore after she'd died because the very thought of his second heart hurt him too much. I did not realize I was staring into the shop until the baker came out to ask if I was alright. I apologized to the man, nodding as I walked away. I was so occupied with my thoughts that I did not realize my name was being called.

"Aleron Aragon!"

I turned to my full name for the second time that night, wondering who it was, to see a boy around ten running towards me.

"Yes? That's me," I answered.

The boy handed me a piece of thick yellow paper. "This is for you."

I took it hesitantly, opening the folded paper and read:

"This is your final warning, Aleron. I know what you are trying to find. Stop. There will be consequences if you fail to do so. I know who you are, I know who you love. I would hate for your dear father to get hurt."

The blood in my veins froze at the words this person had sent me. There was no signature. The writing was flawless.

"Who is this from!" I questioned, tearing my eyes from the paper to see I was alone once again. I spun in a circle, trying to tap down my panic. The boy had disappeared. He was probably a street rat anyway, but I still felt weary. Was he connected somehow, or just a paid messenger boy? Something about his face was familiar to me, but I could not remember where. I re-read the letter, swallowing thickly as my eyes roamed over the sentence that threatened my father.

My walk home had me constantly looking over my shoulder. I shoved the letter in my pocket and tried to keep my worry and panic to a minimum. The letter scared me more than I cared to admit. When I reached for my doorknob my hand was shaking. Before walking into the house, I stood on my porch and shook out my hands, probably looking like an *imbécile*. I did not care. The letter in my pocket seemed to burn a hole through my pants, making my skin burn with the threat that was written on it, imprinting it onto my soul. I twisted the doorknob, walking into the dimly lit room. The fireplace held dying embers in it. I bit my lip. My father was home after all, and it was well after my curfew. The night sky already started to rise by the time I had come up on my house.

"Good evening Al," My father's voice came from behind me. I turned, trepidation filling me as I saw my father sitting at the table, leaning back with his arms crossed. His face was terrifyingly angry. "Where were you today, and before you lie to me, I already know you skipped school." He stood up, shoving his chair back with a screech and slammed a hand down on the table making me jump. "Tell me son, why you were not in school today! Do you even know what day it is?"

"I-I…" I stuttered, I had no way to tell the truth without bringing him into it, the note burning brighter with its warning. I ended up shaking my head. "I'm sorry."

"Sorry is not good enough Al!" My father yelled at me, his face angrier that I had seen it in a long time.

51

"I did not mean to!", I protested. "I was with Clarisse, and I lost track of time." My answer did not seem to appease my father. He was not usually angry or mean, but this was something I had not seen before. I had never seen his jaw so clenched, his shoulders so hunched, or his eyes so painfilled. "What day is it?", I asked softly, hoping with everything in me that I was wrong.

"March seventeenth," My father said softly, his eyes dropping to the table, as he sagged back into his seat.

I closed my eyes in despair, leaning back against the wall, sinking down until I hit the floor. I had missed my mother's death anniversary.

***

"I'm sorry," I whispered thickly, the floor long having gone cold where I sat. My eyes were closed, my hands in my lap, as I leaned my head against the wall. The house was silent. Just our breathing being the only thing I heard. Shame and hurt rippled through me as I thought about what I had missed. Every year on the day my mother died, my father and I went to her grave, picked her favorite wildflowers to put on it, and sometimes my father would tell me more about her. It was a tradition we always did together, each using the other's strength to get through the sadness. I did not know what else to say to him. I did not dare say what I was really doing lest he find out and become hurt. My father's voice dragged me out of my musings.

"Eleven years, Al. She'll be gone eleven years now," My father whispered brokenly. This day was always hard for him, it tore at his heart to see his love buried in the ground while he still lived. When my mother had first became sick, he had held out for a sliver of hope, but when she kept getting worse, my father just caved in on himself. He loved her far more than himself.

I clenched my jaw as I tried to picture my mother's face and failed.

"What were you doing that was so important that you missed today?", My father questioned, turning his brown eyes on me.

I turned my head and looked at him. I licked my lips before answering. For once I said truthfully, "I cannot tell you."

My father's frown deepened, "What do you mean you cannot tell me?"

I stood up, looking at my father pleadingly. I took a seat across from him. "I *cannot* tell you. You will get hurt."

He blew out a harsh breath through his nose. "Aleron! What are you talking about? Are you in some kind of trouble?"

I looked down at the wood table, my fingernail playing with one of the chips in the boards. I said nothing more.

My father looked at me before sighing and pressing his palms into his eyes so hard I thought he was going to hurt himself. "Hell, Aleron," He sighed out, his voice muffled and filled with frustration. "Fine." He looked up at me, with a stern face. "Fine, keep your secrets. I am going to bed." With that he turned off the lamp and picked it up, taking it with him as he walked to his bedroom.

I watched him leave, and the room flooded with darkness once the lamp was gone, and I put my arms on the table, pillowing my head on them. I did not care if a tear or two fell from my eyes. I ended up falling asleep there, guilt eating at me and entering my dreams like an unseen monster.

***

The following week, my father and I were avoiding one another. It seemed I was avoiding a lot of people in my life right now. I stuck to my schedule for a while to appease him. School in the morning, apprenticing for Alex, then coming home. That was it. I did not even see Clarisse for three days before she confronted me about what had happened. Val and Tomas were nowhere to be seen. I saw my uncle give me concerned glances, whenever he was home from working on the Eiffel project. He noticed the tension between my father and I. He had mourned for his sister, but he also did not have a constant reminder of her like my father did, through me.

When I could, I would interview other people on the Committee list. Most of my days I came home exhausted after dark. The people on the list were mostly rich, nobler people. Others were poorer, like me. Some had families, and others were single. There were some who did not really care about Eiffel or the Tower, more willing to just be in the trend of things. I had interviewed a few who were valiant enough to tell me their thoughts about Eiffel, but when I asked them plain outright if they wanted Eiffel dead or hurt most were appalled I had asked such a thing. The men and women of this list were either clueless to the actual threat or only had a slight dislike towards Gustave. I had only gotten through a tenth of the list, maybe thirty people, by the time the end of the week arrived.

I was crossing out another name on the list, using my knee as a firm surface, just having finished asking more meaningless questions to a woman and her husband. They did not even know Gustave Eiffel had rumors about an assassination. I was there when the letter's warning came true. My head shot up as I heard feet running towards me.

My uncle stood there looking panicked, flustered, out of breath, and most of all...scared.

"Uncle Francois?" I asked cautiously, taking a step towards him. "What happened? What's wrong?"

My uncle swallowed, trying to catch his breath. "It is your father." He breathed; his eyes wide.

Before he said anything else, I took off running towards him, with my uncle's call ringing in my ears. I stuck the list in my pocket, that cursed list, and ran so fast dirt was kicking up from my feet digging into the ground. My newsboy hat flew off as I skirted a corner of a building, skidding in the dirt before I took a sort of stumble and kept running. My breath was coming up short and my chest was tight, but I did not dare stop.

I do not know how my uncle had found me but I was so glad he did. My feet were bounding on the ground, and my heartbeat and breathing were the only things I could hear. I should have listened for *once* in my life. If I lost him...

My feet created little trenches in the ground as I stopped in front of my house. My chest heaved as I struggled to take in full breaths. My neighbors, the Devaux family and the Perrys, were all crowded on my porch. The Alixs, Clarisse's family, were also there, meaning the news had already traveled.

Clarisse broke away from the group, with a bonnet on her head, dressed properly unlike the last time we met. She was the first to notice me. "Aler-"

I cut her off. "Is he alive?" I took in a shaky breath. "Just tell me he is alive."

She nodded, putting a hand on my bicep. "He is alive."

I pushed past her and through the small mob, walking into my house. I stopped short at the physician that was tending to my father, his bedroom door open. Mrs. Devaux, an older woman in her sixties, grey hair and kind-faced, took my arm. While I stood there shell shocked she led me towards my father.

"Best to be with him right now, love." She said softly, rubbing a hand down my arm.

I took a seat, numb, as I looked at my injured father laying down in his bed. The physician held a mercury thermometer in his mouth, getting a read on it. My father's eyes were closed, the dark bruises on his face standing out against the white pallor of his skin. He was in his white cotton sleep shirt, which only made him look paler. He had a split lip, bruises around his jaw and temple. My hands gripped the bottom of my chair tightly as I asked the doctor, "What happened?"

The physician, Dr. Victor Paulor, was the closest doctor to my neighborhood for miles. To have him called in was serious. He was white haired, in his mid-seventies, still in good health, with a large white mustache and the bedside manner of a dead mouse. I remembered him from the last time he'd come to my family's home, when my mother was diagnosed with cholera.

Dr. Paulor took out the thermometer and shook it, frowning at the reading. "He was attacked," he started, taking my father's pulse. "He has a concussion, a few bruised ribs, two broken, and several contusions on his face and torso. François found him coming home from work." The doctor explained to me. "I gave him some morphine for the pain and fever. He's sleeping right now."

A hand was petting my head, smoothing down my hair, Mrs. Devaux was a grandmother clearly showing me some of that grandmotherly attention. "When will he wake up?", I asked, refusing to let my voice shake.

I heard another pair of footsteps enter. My uncle's worried form stood beside me. His hand landed reassuringly on my shoulder. "It might take a while Al, maybe by tomorrow morning. His body is healing," my uncle managed to say.

I sat there looking at my father, guilt coming up and gripping my heart like a vice. The doctor and my uncle left the room, talking about payment, as I scooted closer in the chair to my *père*. Mrs. Devaux fixed a small cloth dipped in cool water and placed it against my father's forehead. His brown, shoulder-length hair was pulled to one shoulder. It was usually pulled back. To see it loose was odd.

"I will let you two loves have some privacy," She said, giving my shoulder a squeeze before she left and closed the door behind her.

Swallowing my emotions down as I thanked her and took my father's limp hand in mine I started talking. "I'm sorry," I choked out. "I cannot lose you, *père*. This is all my fault." I brought my forehead down to touch his hand, half of my body leaning against his bed. My body shook with repressed sobs. My throat closing with worry, anguish, guilt, fear, everything. "I can't...I'm sorry, it's my fault. I will be a better son. You are all I have left," I admitted, warm, salty tears falling down my cheeks. I stared at his cream-colored bedding, holding his hand in both of mine. "I love you. Please be okay. Please don't...please," I begged, putting his hand against my cheek, scared out of my mind. Whoever had given me the letter was out there to get me. They made good on their word. They knew where I lived, who I loved, and they knew my father was so important to me. This was not a game anymore. It was real. The realization shook me badly, almost as much as seeing my father stark white and unmoving in his bed. I cried for a while, as my heart was aching with the thought of leaving my father and I's relationship so strained and painful. A concussion was serious, and broken ribs even more so. If he got an infection and died....it would be on me. I could not bury another parent. I do not know how long I stayed awake, but by the time I closed my eyes dawn was breaking. A hand brushed my hair back from where I was leaning my head on the bed, eyes closed and no doubt puffy and red. My eyes shot open when I registered the movement.

"Father?", I mumbled, blinking away the slight twinges of sleep I had.

"That's me," My father answered, his voice course and low from disuse. He looked at me, his brown eyes tired but warm, a small smile on his face as his hand brushed my hair back. So much more comforting than Mrs. Devaux's. A parent's touch always felt that way. I simply stared at him, seeing him awake and coherent, a blessing in and of itself.

My lip trembled and my shoulders slumped as I carefully threw myself onto my father, giving him a hug. Throwing my arm over his shoulder, I tucked my head into his neck. "I'm sorry, I'm sorry for everything." Those words seemed to be the only ones I could say anymore.

My father shushed me, like I was six again and climbing into his bed after a nightmare. "It is alright Al, everything's alright."

58

I sobbed against his shoulder, relief so overwhelming I felt lightheaded. My tears had turned into ones of surrender, as I hugged my father, thankful he was going to be alright. I realized that this was too much. I had to quit. My family and loved ones could not get hurt. I knew that I was on the right path, otherwise I would not be getting threatened, but my father was more important than a stranger, my uncle, or even Clarisse. I felt sorry for Eiffel, but I hardened my resolve... I was done.

Investigation closed.

Chapter Six - Mon EnquêteFermé

My investigation closed, I had nothing more to do then focus on helping my father heal. I took all the papers that Eiffel had given me, the telegram that my uncle had, with any other notes that I had written or gotten and stuffed all of it into a box. I shoved it under my bed. I forced myself to forget about it as I stayed home and helped my father get better. He was bedridden by the doctor's orders to heal his ribs — moving wasn't much of an option at the moment. My uncle helped when he could, but the project and construction of the Eiffel Tower was something that took up his day and he came home exhausted from working on blueprints with the other builders. It was left to me.

I would wake up early in the morning, with the rising sun of dawn, and make my family some type of breakfast. There was not much I couldn't burn. My mother had been the cook of the family. I would head to school, most of the day I was distracted by my ideas about Eiffel. I came home with welts on the skin of my wrists from *Monsieur* Ennuyeux's ruler for lack of attention. I was distracted with my grandeur thoughts about the assassination plot, as well as trying to avoid Clarisse, Tomas, and Val. It was difficult to carry the hidden burden that plagued my thoughts by disregarding the rumors. Guilt was eating at me so strongly that some days I struggled to get out of bed. I barely apprenticed for Alex during the day, I was sure he noticed but he respected my privacy.

I was eating breakfast a few days later with my father. Still bedridden but getting better; when he made me sit down and he talked some sense into me.

"Aleron, what's going on? You're not acting your usual self," He told me, placing a hand on my bicep. "I'm going to be fine soon, don't worry about that."

I smiled sadly. I still hadn't told him what was going on. "I'm fine *père*," I stirred my porridge with a slightly burnt piece of bread.

"Al," My father sighed. "For once in your life, can you tell me the truth?"

I held back the hurt that I felt from his words— they were true. I looked down at the beige colored food I had made and slowly my eyes filled with tears, not that I wanted them to, but all of the feelings that I'd experienced started spilling over. I could tell my father didn't expect this because he was very silent.

Once I had managed to draw in a few deep breaths, the tears subsided, and I was able to tell my father the truth. "It's my fault," I answered. "I did something to cause this and now people I love are in danger." I whispered, shame coloring my cheeks. I excused myself and quickly grabbed the box of papers

I had stuffed under my bed. I hadn't looked at it in over a week. Coming back to my father I placed the box in his lap. "This is everything I've uncovered." I explained at his confused look.

"In…" He asked, opening the box and pulling out papers.

"In the investigation of the assassination plot of Gustave Eiffel," I managed to say, not meeting my father's eye.

"Aleron…" He started, trailing off as he looked at the papers. The list of names, most crossed off, the handwritten notes I had made, newspaper clippings — the whole lot of it. "So... you *did* hear your uncle and I, didn't you?" He finally said.

I nodded my head, standing up and pacing as I explained. "I couldn't let it be. Uncle wasn't going to do anything with the information. He doesn't even really like Eiffel." I spun towards my father, "Most people think it's a rumor...but something in me is *screaming* that this can't be left alone. I went and met Eiffel, he's scared Father. I could read it in his eyes." I didn't tell him that Eiffel had the same look on his face that my mother did when she was told her diagnosis. That same sliver of hope that's barely there, but the overall acceptance that death might be coming for them. "When I got this, I stopped. I couldn't lose anyone else." I said as I pulled out the warning letter from the bottom on the box. Shoved all the way down to the bottom and crumpled on purpose. I showed it to my father, who paled a little, his already ashen face taking a sickly white tone that made me anxious.

He read the words and put the paper down after a moment. Looking me in the eye he ordered, "Tell me everything."

I did. I told him from the very moment I overheard him and Uncle François talk about the assassination, to the accident two weeks ago which landed him in his bed with broken ribs. I told him about my fight with Tomas and Val, how Clarisse wanted

61

and still wants to help. I explained my visit to Eiffel, plus the terrible visit to Charles Garnier. In the end I was exhausted from my explanation, reliving all of the events in the past few weeks had taken a toll on my heart and subconscious. Closing my eyes as I waited for my father to say something...anything. I was filled with the scary thought that because I finally told someone what was going on, the person that had threatened my father would come again for a second attempt on his life.

"*Père?*" I asked, opening my eyes to see my father looking at me.

"Aleron..."

I braced myself for a scolding, but the gentle hand on my knee startled me.

"Al, I'm so proud of you."

Those were not the words I was expecting. "W-what?" I stammered.

My father smiled, "I'm proud of you Al, this is amazing work." His face softened and turned somber. "I'm sorry you felt like you couldn't come to me with this. I'm sure this is a lot to handle on your shoulders."

I shrugged. I had large shoulders; I could carry a certain amount of weight. I had been doing it since I was six, my mother had large shoulders too. She was stronger than I ever could be. "What do we do now?" I thought aloud, "I must have been on the right tract, otherwise I wouldn't have gotten threatened like I did. Whoever's behind this is after me."

My father bristled at this, probably hating the thought that his child was in danger.

"Well, there's a little more than a month left before the World's Fair so whatever they're planning they're going to be doing it soon. *Mon Dieu*, this is really happening." He answered, as he touched his forehead.

I could tell he was getting tired, so I carefully tucked everything back into the box and set it on the floor while I pushed back my chair. "You should probably be resting, Father. We'll decide what to do when you're feeling better." I suggested, fluffing his flat pillow behind him.

"I can ask some of my colleagues if they've heard anything. I'm sure a few of their wives have heard the town *potins*. Sometimes a group of women whose tongues waggle know more about the town they live in then the President of France."

I chuckled a little as my father compared Sadi Carnot, the President of France, to a group of town gossips. "But you're just a teacher," I pointed out. "How can you find out such information?"

My father quirked an eyebrow. "I might be *just* a teacher Al, but you'd be surprised what your father can accomplish. Don't give up, *mon garçon préféré*." He left it at that as his eyes closed and he patted my hand to dismiss me.

Letting my father rest, I picked up the dishes we made dirty and closed his door. His nickname was one that he hadn't used in years, mostly because my mother would say it. I was her favorite boy. The phrase always said playfully in front of my father, I wondered why he decided to use it now. I put my box back into my room for safe keeping.

There was still plenty of daylight left in the day and since I had nothing more to do, I decided to head somewhere I shouldn't have gone to in the first place. Eiffel was due another visit. Grabbing my bike, I peddled quickly to his hotel, this time asking truthfully if Eiffel was in. The clerk told me he was and so I made my way up the stairs, taking a breath before knocking on his door; having just noticed the number twelve on the door was slightly crooked. I hadn't noticed it the first time I was there. When there was no answer, I panicked, knocking on the door harder than before. It finally opened and I let out a breath of relief until I saw Gustave face to face.

"Monsieur.... what happened?", I asked, slightly shell shocked at the sight before me. I opened the door a little more with my arm, staring at the most controversial face in Paris. I was alarmed to see one of his eyes nearly swollen shut. It was black and blue and looked painful to touch. His prominent Roman nose was now slightly crooked and clearly broken. He had a gash on his cheekbone and one near his temple, his arm was in a cloth sling, tied around his neck. The words that I had fully prepared in my mind left my head.

Eiffel sighed and opened the door fully. "Better come in Al," He managed before shuffling to sit gingerly down in his chair almost identical to the first time we had talked. I could tell from his body language that he most likely had injuries like my father. The dreadful experience of having spikes of pain shoot through you every time you breathed.

I'd experienced a few broken ribs from my fights at school. Oh, how those days seemed so long ago compared to where I was now. I was also surprised that he'd remembered my name. "Are you all right?" I asked, coming down and sitting across from him.

Before Eiffel could respond, a third voice came from the corner of the room, where Eiffel's friend, Maurice Koechlin, was pouring the men stiff drinks. "My friend here got beaten up by some *fauteurs de troubles,*" The man spit out, handing the drink to his friend. "I found him and called the doctor. The stubborn man wouldn't give up descriptions to the authorities." Maurice slapped a hand on his friend's shoulder. "Insisted he wanted the whole thing to be kept under wraps." He went and stood near the window, the setting sun illuminating his silhouette.

I shifted in my chair from Maurice to Gustave, "You were attacked too?" I asked, aghast. This definitely wasn't a coincidence. My father and Gustave Eiffel getting attacked within days of each other? No, whoever was behind the assassination plot was also behind this.

"Too?" Eiffel inquired, taking a small sip of his drink. "Who else was attacked, my boy?"

I hesitated in answering, my gaze turning to *Monsieur* Koechlin. I did not know who to trust at this moment, friend of Eiffel's or not. I took a moment and looked at Maurice, studying him carefully. The clothes he was wearing were nice, clearly an intelligent French man's suit, but Eiffel's suit still looked like it cost more. His short beard and mustache were as dark as the receding hair on the top of his head. His face was thin, almost skeletal. His eyes glittered like dark stones, I held back a shiver, in the light they looked almost pitch black. Soulless. His gaze met mine and I couldn't help tearing my eyes away to look back at Eiffel.

Eiffel noticed my hesitancy. "Don't worry about Maurice here," He stood up and clapped the man on the back roughly, making his friend take a step forward. "He's as loyal as a dog. He's been working with me on the Tower, in fact he's one of my top engineers and architects."

Maurice gave Gustave a tight smile, wiping his hand on a clothe from where he'd spilled his drink because of Gustave's hearty slap on the back. "Thank you, Gustave."

Eiffel laughed deeply, but what was funny I did not know. He came back and sat down across from me again. Nodding his head towards me he said, "Aleron, please tell us what's happened. Nothing too bad I hope?" He grinned before taking a sip.

"My father was attacked," I started.

Eiffel choked on his drink, coughing harshly as he looked at me with wide eyes on his round face, the back of his hand over his mouth for a moment. "*Mon Dieu*, so it *is* true."

"A few days before you, as it seems," I added, once Eiffel was able to take a normal breath again. "I was on the right trail," I admitted.

Maurice sat down on a third chair, closest to the window, leaning forward with interest. "What is true?" He asked.

"The rumors." Both Eiffel and I answered in unison.

Eiffel nodded for me to take the lead and so I told them what I had accomplished, what I had found out, the letter and the note that threatened my family. When I finished there was a silence that filled the room, suffocating me.

Eiffel suddenly stood up, startling me, and began pacing the room while Maurice stared into his drink. Both in deep thought.

"There must be something we can do to stop this," Maurice offered, looking at me with a pleading gaze. "Eiffel has been my friend for years; I don't see why anyone would want to hurt him."

"This is deplorable, Aleron. I'm deeply sorry your father got hurt because of this." Eiffel told me, stopping his pacing for a moment. "We could take this to the authorities. *Le poste de police*, perhaps."

I shook my head, I had gone to the police already, they had brushed it off as nothing more than rumors. "I've tried," I shrugged my shoulders. "They didn't believe me."

"But you have proof now, your letters at home, the telegram! If you should give it to them maybe they could look into it." Eiffel pointed out, holding his aching arm close to his chest. "*J'ai mal à la tête,* my head is pounding from all this nonsense.*" He said, touching a hand to his temple.

"It's worth a try to go again, if it means saving your life *Monsieur*." I acknowledged. "I have the papers at home, I'll bring them to the police first thing tomorrow morning." I'd promise myself that I would stop the investigation, but seeing my father willing to help, seeing Eiffel hurt and roughed up and seeing that I was getting closer to the answer... I couldn't stop, I couldn't let Eiffel die. It was my mission now, however reluctant I was, I was fully tied into this whole debacle.

Eiffel looked into my face, reading mine and I clearly read his. Never had I seen a grown man look more like a lost little boy in his inner self. I felt pity for what Eiffel was going through, the stress and fear that every moment could possibly be your last. No knowing who was after you or how to stop them. I did not envy him.

"Thank you Aleron, you don't know how much this means to me that you're trying to stop this." He finally managed to say. Gustave chuckled mirthlessly, "I can't say that many are willing to do so." Taking a seat, he sighed heavily. "*Bonne chance à toi,* Aleron. *Que Dieu soit avec vous.*"

I took his wish of good luck and for God to be with me to heart. I nodded my thanks and stood up. *"Merci,"* I headed towards the door. "I best be going home. It's growing late."

"Oui," Maurice agreed, walking towards the door as well. "We'll let you rest, Eiffel. *Au revoir mon ami."*

"Au revoir," I copied, both of us taking our leave.

Monsieur Koechlin stopped me with a hand to my shoulder once the door was closed.

I looked up at him, "Sir?"

His face turned soft. "Please help my friend Aleron. I could tell that he doesn't want this to go public. It would ruin his project and his reputation. The only thing he cares about is that damned project of his. The Eiffel Tower. Aleron, be *careful* about this," He warned, his hand tightening just a smidge.

I nodded. *"Merci,"* Something in me wanted to ask him why he hadn't done anything to help his friend if he was so worried, but I kept my mouth shut. I had no place to judge, perhaps he had helped in some way. Fate had decided this was my task, a monumental one, but I was willing to be saddled with it. I only hoped it worked out for the good. With barely a month left before the World's Fair I had to put everything I had into this investigation. That would include putting my friends and family at risk. I swallowed my anxiety and bid the man good night.

The night sky was turning twilight as I headed back home, peddling over the loose gravel and dirt roads. There was barely anyone out and the night was still. I swear that even the wind and air were asleep. Every so often a lamp post would light my way as I peddled home.

Parking my bike by the side of my house, I opened the door slowly and quietly, stepping over certain floorboards I knew would squeak. I checked on my father and uncle, both of them asleep in their own rooms. It was late, much later than my father would have let me be out if he were fully well and awake. I headed to my room and stopped short.

I shook my head. *"Je t'en prie, non,"* I pleaded, rushing forward and dropping to my knees. The box...the papers, all of them were in shreds, I scrambled to search for the letter, the telegram, the note, anything proof worthy. There was nothing, *nothing.* My heart sank into my stomach and bile filled my mouth. I put a hand against my chest as my breaths started coming shorter and faster. Someone had been in my house, in my *room.* They'd found my box of information, under my bed no less, taking it apart and left it for me to find. I shivered at the thought that someone evil knew where I lived, could get into my room while my father and uncle slept nearby. I felt petrified with fear, worry making my hands shake and head spin. I checked the papers one more time, hoping beyond hope but, they knew exactly what they were looking for. My uncle's telegram, gone. The newspaper clippings — gone. Eiffel's list of names — gone. It was all gone. I blinked wearily at the box, numb to any feeling. They knew exactly when to come too. My father had been otherwise occupied, my uncle out of the house. Myself out on my investigation… They must have been watching the house. All incriminating evidence I once had….gone. What was I supposed to take to the authorities now? I didn't sleep that night. The moon shone down with its melancholy light on a scene that was filled with sorrow, the only witness to what had been committed.

***

69

The rising sun blared into my eyes, it seemed to be the only thing that woke me up from my trance-like state. I'd simply stared out my window, stuck in my unbelief of what had happened. I gathered my courage, going to draw my window's curtain firmly closed when I spotted something. I looked curiously at the shred of blue fabric I plucked off an upturned nail head.

Plucking it off I looked at it, feeling it between my fingers. It was a soft blue piece of fabric. Whoever had come into my room had torn their clothing on the way out. That sure helped....dozens of people wore blue in just my town alone, much less the whole of Paris.

I threw it angrily on the floor, storming out of my room. My father met me in the parlor, still looking pained from his ribs but needing the change of scenery from his room. Much like me, my father was not one to stay still for long.

"It's gone." I cried, stilling him with my look.

"What are gone, Al?", My Uncle asked, coming into the room with the morning's newspaper.

I bit my lip looking at my father for approval, wondering if I should share with my uncle. After all, he was technically the one that started me on this journey. My father nodded and we both took a moment to fill my uncle in, telling him everything I had learned as well as the cause of Eiffel's and my father's attacks.

"The notes, the letters, they're gone," I explained afterwards. "Someone took them while I was gone, while you were asleep."

My Uncle François looked practically distraught. "This is all my fault," he said softly. "If I hadn't gotten that *maudit*telegram." He bit out, putting his head in his hand.

I slapped my own forehead, suddenly wondering why I had never asked this question before. "Uncle, where did you even *get* the telegram?"

My uncle shook his head, "I don't know," he answered. "It was simply sent to me, I asked, and they didn't know who had sent it, only that it was for me."

I slumped in defeat; the lead I was hoping for vanished before it had even begun. I took in a calming breath and let it out slowly. "I promised *Monsieur* Eiffel I would try. I have to go to the police; I might have nothing to show them, but I at least need to try." I clenched my fists in anger at the thought that someone had tried to stop me again. I snatched my newsboy hat off its peg on the wall. "I'm going now, time is already running out, and I know that whoever is behind this is *more* than willing to stick to their word." I opened the door when my father called out.

"Aleron, wait," He stood up and grabbed his coat. "Let us help. Three accusations are better than one."

I gave my father a thankful look, smiling both at both my uncle and father gratefully, "Thank you."

My uncle nodded. "You'll be sure that I'll ask around the others at the construction site. They might be of use to get us some information."

With that, the three of us made our way across town, getting a coach because my father couldn't walk that far. We got to the police station, greeted by an officer at the front desk. His young face made me hopeful that he would listen to us rather than the rumors that were currently floating around. His uniform was new looking, the brass buttons shiny and still copper colored. His dark blue uniform was intimidating, the black *kepi* hat he was wearing shadowed his face.

"*Bonjour*, what can I help you with?" he asked, lifting his eyes from the paperwork in front of him.

"*Bonjour*," I started. I thought for a moment before I decided the best way would to just be blunt. "We would like to report a crime."

My words got a lift of a brow and a peaked interest. "What kind of crime?" The officer asked, bringing out what looked like a report and a graphite pencil.

"An assassination." I answered, placing my hands down on his desk, praying he believed me.

The officer sighed heavily, putting away the pencil and paper. Steepling his hands together, he gave me a stern look. "If this is about Eiffel and his *supposed* assassination, then I will not hear another word about it."

I shook my head, "Please, sir…"

He cut me off. "Eiffel is all we hear about anymore," His voice turned hard. "Do you have proof?"

My shoulders slumped and I breathed a harsh breath through my nose. "No, not any-"

I got cut off again. "Then we're through, when you have proof you may come back," The man said.

"No!" I protested. "A man's life is in danger, do you not care? You should at least look into it!"

The man stood up, getting into my face. "People die in this city every day, I don't care if it happens to be a famous architect." He slapped the desk, "Now listen here, boy," He stuck a finger in my face, and I resisted the urge to break it. "We police deal with everything this city throws at us including riots, thefts, people getting robbed, murders, bombs, thugs, and everything in between. And you know what we get in return? A measly four *francs* and seventy-five cents for an eleven and a half-hour day." He sneered at me. "I don't have time to investigate every damn rumor a single *imbécile*comes up with." The officer sat down, our discussion apparently over.

I clenched my jaw so hard I heard it crack, as my nose scrunched into a growl. Before I could say anything, my father put a hand against my arm and shook his head. The angry, hurtful words I had on my tongue died away at his look. Getting stuck in jail or arrested was not going to help Eiffel. Or myself for that matter.

I tugged my arm out of my father's grip and stormed out of the building. I clomped down the stairs, I was so angry that I was surprised the cool breeze wasn't thawing from the steam that was coming out of my ears.

"Aleron? What are you doing here?" I heard the familiar voice of Clarisse ask, I turned and she stared at me.

"It was something to do with Eiffel, Clarisse." I admitted after a moment's hesitation of staring into her eyes. The bonnet and beige dress she was wearing highlighted her pale skin, seeing her again loosened something in my chest. Knowing that she was alright strengthened me. Without thinking I crossed over to her and hugged her.

She stiffened for a moment before allowing herself to give me a small hug back. "Al?" Clarisse asked cautiously. "What's wrong?" she pulled back out of my grip.

I let her go, knowing that it wasn't proper for an unmarried lady to hug a man in public, but wishing the hug had lasted a little longer. "The police won't investigate."

"What?" Clarisse gasped, mouth dropping open. "How can they do that?"

I shook my head, re-sparking my anger. "They said they wouldn't do anything until I have proof."

"But you do!" She pointed out, gripping my arm.

Shaking my head sadly I said, "No, not anymore."

Her face turned crestfallen, "Why not, what happened?"

"Someone came into my house, into my room, found the box and shredded my papers. Taking the notes, threats, and original telegram with them," I took off my cap rubbing my hand through my hair before placing it back on. "I was too late to stop them."

"Oh Aleron," Clarisse comforted, voice soft and angelic.

I turned towards my father and uncle, who were just coming down the few steps of the station. Their subtle shakes of their heads telling me that they hadn't gotten any further with the policeman than I did. "I'll see you later Clarisse, *Au revior.*"

Clarisse waved softy as the three of us left. "*Au revoir.* I'm so sorry."

I looked back seeing tears in her eyes. Forcing myself not to run to her to comfort her, I continued walking.

Perhaps a little bit harsher than normal, but neither my uncle nor father said anything about it.

I didn't know what to do now, again it was up to me. Other than the two men following me home apparently no one else cared enough to help Gustave Eiffel.

∗∗∗

The following day my father went back to work for the first time in three weeks. He promised to ask around the school and the teachers to see if anyone knew anything. My uncle went to work, same as every other day while I simmered in animosity and anger. I went to school because of my father's instance, the first one out when it ended, storming my way to Alex's shop. I hadn't seen him in a week, my friend had given me a much-needed break from my apprentice duties at his shop, something I'd be forever grateful for.

The door jingled with the little bells that Alex had put above the door. I went ahead and put on my clerk's apron, calling out his name. "Alex! Where are you?" It was quiet, which was bizarre. The shop was always alive with either Alex, myself, or whatever ticking project Alex was tinkering with — something was different. It was *too* quiet. Slipping into the back I called for my friend again. "Alex?!" I went and searched the back room, his desk was empty, messy as usual. My heart pounded in my chest. Alex was like an older brother to me, a better friend than most, I couldn't drag him into this as well. I tore off my apron, dashing out the door, not even bothering to lock up. I ran as fast as I could towards where I hoped he'd be.

Mon Dieu, what was I doing, dragging everyone that I cared about into this…? I was going to hurt people through this…what if someone died…. because of me.

My feet ran faster as I pumped my arms harder, coming within view of the Tower's construction, knowing that Alex would probably be watching or maybe even involved knowing how curious he was. If anything happened to that glasses-wearing, loveable fool, an old friend to both my mother and father, I'd never forgive myself. I shoved my way through groups of men carrying poles, men working with metal, looking for a brown head of hair and owl-like glasses.

"Alex!" I yelled relief flooding my chest at spotting him. I started rushing forward, I needed to see him, hug him like I did with Clarisse to reassure myself he was alright. *Alive.*

"Aleron?" My friend yelled, turning away from the men he was talking to, a quizzical look on his face even from where I was, I could see it.

 He saw my urgency and took a few steps towards me. "What's wrong?" he shouted.

I made my way towards him, pushing past people when a viciously loud groan was heard, the sound of metal creaking. My eyes darted everywhere as I stilled, looking for where the sound was coming from. My gaze landed on a large metal beam with wood boards on top hanging from thick ropes, being pulled up to be used. I heard one of them snap. It echoed through my ears like a gunshot. My gaze traveled down…. Alex was standing directly underneath the beam. Please no… I willed my body to move but my legs had turned to lead, my blood freezing in fear. Another snap spurned me into action. I nearly tripped in my haste to get to my friend. There was such a distance between us — it was too far. I knew it in my soul. Desperately, I called out. "Alex! Move!"

Instead of moving away, he took a step closer. "What are you doing?" He asked, shouting louder.

I waved my arm to the side. "Get out of the way! *Move.*" Another snap preceded my words, that terrible groaning roaring loudly. I was within twenty feet of my friend when I saw the rope snap completely. I reached an arm out to him. "Alex, nooo!", I screamed, the words tearing themselves free from my throat. The beam fell with a crash, the groan of metal, the snap of bone, the splintering of wood...Alex's yell...

Chapter Seven - Cher Dieu

"Dear God..." I heard someone say as I skidded on my knees through the dirt to the pile of material that was covering my friend...

I was seconds too late... seconds.

I yelled as I strained to lift up the beam, my feet digging into the dirt as I drew in a ragged breath, trying not to cry or yell. My action spurred other men into action. Apparently seeing a seventeen-year-old boy be the first one to help wounded men's pride. I heard someone yell for a medic or a doctor, I couldn't fully tell. The only thing I could hear was my heartbeat in my ears, my panting breaths coming out too harshly. I prayed, I begged, I hoped, that Alex was alive somehow. That he was still breathing under that rubble. Working quickly with the other men we managed to uncover him...my stomach turned inside out as I noticed the blood. So much blood. The thick red liquid pooled in a spot big enough where I could see my own terrified reflection. I nearly heaved but managed to keep it down by squeezing my thumb into my fist, something my mother showed me once.

Was Alex greeting her as we spoke? I could not even begin to think like that.

I was shoved out of the way by a doctor. The first thing he did was to look for a pulse…

I swallowed my breaths until he yelled Alex was alive. I felt myself list to the side — my knees collapsing. I landed roughly in the dirt, catching myself on my hand. I felt faint, everything blurry and muffled. I blinked sluggishly as fingers snapped in front of my face. I squinted...I knew those fingers.

"U-uncle Francois?" I mumbled. I was delirious with the relief that I felt in knowing Alex was alive. Hurt yes, but alive. At the moment that was all that mattered.

My uncle was crouching down in front of me, trying to get my attention by yelling my name. He was blocking my view, but not entirely. The image of Alex's bloody body, his left leg clearly gone from the calf down and wrapped with soaking red bandages being carried away on a stretcher, would forever stay in my mind. My blinks seemed to take seconds to accomplish as I saw my friend carried off. I sluggishly looked back at my uncle, slumping against his chest before I knew nothing more than the numbness that came with darkness. Alex's yell still repeated as I lost consciousness.

When I woke up I simply stared at my ceiling. At first, I didn't recall how I had gotten in my own bed, what had happened…. But then I remembered. Shooting straight up I threw the covers off of me and stood up. I swayed as my vision went black, my knees weak.

"Whoa, easy there Al, take it easy." My Uncle's voice became clear after the ringing left. "You're going to need a minute, after not sleeping for an entire day and skipping two meals it wasn't hard to figure out why you lost consciousness." His gentle hand righting me at my shoulder gave a reassuring squeeze.

I looked up at him, brushing a stray strand of hair away from my face. "Alex?" I wanted to know what had happened, if he was alive… if he was okay.

"Alive." My uncle answered, the pressure in my chest loosening slightly with his answer.

"How long have I been out?" I touched my head as pain spiked. Hissing past the pain, I pushed past my uncle. "I need to see him."

"A day. Do you plan on seeing your friend dressed in only your night clothes?" My uncle asked, smirking with a raised eyebrow.

I flushed and looked down, taking in my appearance and the realization that someone had changed me into them. "I'll change and then we can go?" I'd already grabbed some clothes from my trunk at the foot of my bed. Biting my lip, I turned to my uncle. "Who changed my clothes?" If *anyone* had changed my clothes...my face flamed with embarrassment at the thought.

My uncle let out a laugh, "Don't worry Aleron, we woke you up enough to change clothes, but you were so exhausted you passed out again."

I let out a breath of relief, that I could live with. I shooed my uncle out of my room and quickly changed into something more suitable, snapping my suspenders against my chest and grabbed my newsboy hat. My hands were shaking with anxiety and nerves at seeing my friend. He was alive and for that I held onto my belief that he'd be alright.

My uncle walked with me to the physician where Alex was taken. I was worrying my lip the entire journey. By the time we arrived my bottom lip was bleeding from my constant gnawing of it. The physician's place was where people greeted death, wounds were healed, and faces lost hope. I knew from experience. The building had been ingrained in my memory since I was six years old. It was a drab dark building...small. It held the doctor's office, two recovery rooms, and an operating theater. I hesitated at the door, looking up at the sign and struggling not to think about my mother. Eventually my uncle nudged me, and I walked in.

A nurse, her face was pale and guarded, in her sterile blue gown and white cap led us to Alex's room. I wrinkled my nose at the metallic smell of blood and the sharp sting of infection. I took off my hat and fiddled it with my hands. My friend looked like a corpse. He was so still he looked on the verge of death. I had never seen Alex without his glasses on his face. His nose always had creases on the bridge from their weight. Now it looks unnatural to see his sweaty, pale face without his signature feature. I walked over, nearly in a trance, and touched his face with the back of my hand. He was hot to the touch, almost burning. I carefully rearranged the wet, lukewarm cloth on his forehead.

"He has a fever?", I asked, not tearing my eyes away from Alex's chest, which was wrapped and taking small minute breaths of air.

Dr. Paulor, the same man who seemed to be associated with every single hurt person I'd ever loved, looked at me. There were other doctors, how did I get so lucky to keep seeing his face. He answered my question in a gruff voice. "Indeed, he has an infection from the amputated leg."

His words commanded my eyes to travel down, seeing the wrongly ending lump under the crisp white sheets that were covering Alex. My headache spiked as I looked at his missing limb. I felt slightly faint the longer my gaze lingered.

"He also has several broken ribs, some internal bleeding, a concussion, the list goes on." Dr. Paulor added, his voice grating against my ears like nails on a blackboard. The man continued, not taking notice of my agitation.

"We were lucky his ribs didn't pierce his lungs, otherwise..." The man shrugged, his white doctor's coat whispering behind him. "We managed to save his other leg. It's broken but not badly. He's lost a lot of blood. We gave him Morphine and all the whiskey we put in him as we fixed his missing leg should be enough to keep him out for a while."

"How long do you think it will take for him to recover?" My uncle said, his voice soft as he stared at the hurt younger man in the bed. His eyes roaming over my father and I's friend with sympathy.

Again, the reverend doctor shrugged. I was amazed that this man was able to heal anyone with his lack of decorum and bedside manner. "If he gets sepsis then..." he trailed off, looking down at his patient. "We'll do what we can for him," He offered as an answer.

81

I ground my jaw, flaring the pain in my head. Seeing Alex like this...it tore at my heart. "Could we have a moment of privacy?" I asked, turning back to the doctor and my uncle, giving my best pleading face I had.

Dr. Paulor nodded, "*Oui,* you may have a few moments." He left us and closed the door.

I took Alex's limp hand, much like I had with my father all but a few weeks ago. "*Je suis tellement désolé, pardonne-moi.*" I whispered to him, apologizing. Somehow this was connected to my investigation, to Eiffel, to the monster behind all of it. There was already too much suffering that I'd caused. My mother...my father...now Alex. Needing something to do with my hands I soaked his cloth and wrung it out. "It's connected isn't it?"

My uncle sighed, running a hand down his face. "You were always so smart." He took a moment before answering, and I knew then that it was connected. "We looked into the cause of the accident. The ropes were cut. They did not just break on accident. They were already cut into when the beam was pulled up. Your father and I think it's connected. They knew who to target." He clapped a hand on my shoulder, making me give a little grunt. "You probably saved his life Aleron. With you calling to him, if he hadn't taken a few steps forward the beam would have fallen right on top of him. Instead of just getting his legs, he probably would have died. You and your quick thinking, saved him Al."

I couldn't hide the bitter tone my voice held. "If this is what saving him looks like...maybe I shouldn't have." I placed the cloth back on his forehead. I prayed a quick hymn over Alex in my mind, but they had never done any good for my mother, no matter how fervently I asked. If Alex survived, I might think differently, but for now...it was habit only. "I need to end this." I told my uncle, my hard and rough voice not sounding like myself. There was a possibility that in my curiosity, my thirst for adventure...I had essentially killed my friend.

I left after that, unsure if my uncle would follow, but not caring enough to check. My head was ringing by now, probably from lack of food and sleep. The image of seeing Alex so still like that, so hurt and broken wounded me. I felt like I was hearing the news of my father's attack all over again, that same helpless feeling that I hated. I hated all of this. I felt so guilty for letting this happen, for being the cause of it all. I loathed whoever was behind this, cursing them for their vengeance. I hated Clarisse and my feelings for her, I hated Tomas and Val. I hated my uncle who brought this whole thing into my life. I hated myself. Slumping down against the shaded area of a random building, I struggled to reign in my emotions. I thunked my head, hard, against the wall of the building. My headache flared, but I deserved the pain. I did it again and clenched my hands into fists, closing my eyes. I brought forth my anger, my hatred, my malevolence, letting it build in my chest. Shoving down any other emotion, I focused on the one thought of getting answers, of ending the investigation, finding the person behind it and saving Eiffel. Once centered on that and the mix of red that bubbled dangerously in my chest, simply waiting to blow, I opened my eyes. I felt *different*. I got off the floor and dusted my trousers, placing my hat firmly on my head. With purpose in my stride I started off again. There were already enough people that I had let down in my life, I would *not* add Alex to the list.

✳✳✳

I was heading towards Clarisse's house, when I heard a shrill scream. I ran forward, looking for where it was coming from. It was a scared scream, from the pitch I guessed that it came from a woman. My heart jumped into my throat. I was near Clarisse's house, *Mon Dieu,* if….no, not again.… I heard another yell, this time mixed with angry words that I couldn't decipher.

"Clarisse!" I called. My anger burned behind my steps, I stalked towards the sounds of a scuffle. I turned across the street to see a man restraining a woman by gripping her wrists. The woman was struggling to be released, bravely fighting off the man. I couldn't see her face, but I recognized the man. He was the man who Clarisse had talked to, one of her would-be suitors. I didn't even know his name; other than his face I didn't know anything about him.

"You, *Cochon dégoûtant,* get away from her!" I yelled, my voice carrying loudly, rushing towards them. The man looked up startled, his face obscured by his hat. He released the woman and she fell to the ground crying. I trailed after the man, pursuing him until I lost him in a busy street, the few steps ahead of me that he managed to be allowed him to get lost in the busy streets and the crows that surrounded the middle of my small town. I growled in frustration and stomped my foot down. "*Merde!*" I cursed. Suddenly remembering the woman, I rushed back down the streets, ducking down to see her still crying.

"Hey, hey, it's alright," I shushed, putting a gentle hand on her shoulder. Her appearance was disheveled, but she appeared overall unharmed. Her dress was dark blue, smears of dirt on the bottom and sleeves. Her brown hair covering her face as she held a hand against her mouth to stifle the sobs. "Did he hurt you? What's his name?" I questioned.

She shook her head but didn't answer otherwise.

Looking around I spotted her bonnet and dusted it off, "Here," I offered, handing it back to her. I didn't want to push but I need to be sure that she was alright. It was my duty as a gentleman.

She took it, her hands shaky and finally looked up at me. The bright blue eyes that I loved so much met mine. Clarisse's bottom lip trembled as she opened her mouth to speak but more sobs only came out. A handprint stood out wickedly red against the pale skin of her cheek.

"Clarisse," I gasped out, gently thumbing the bruise, "Are you alright, did he hurt you? What did he do to you?"

Clarisse shook her head, "No, h-he did not hurt me." She closed her eyes tightly, "We were talking and he got angry a-and he...he s-slapped me." Her voice broke again and I moved to tuck her under my chin.

"Shh, it's alright. You're safe now, *ma belle*," I comforted her, rubbing my hand down her arm. She continued to cry while I held her in my arms, her tears soaking into my shirt like salty raindrops. I kissed the top of her head as her hand clenched my arm in a comforting grip.

"Clarisse!" I heard another woman call worriedly, coming towards us. I recognized her as Mrs. Alix, Clarisse's mother. Taking in our arrangement, seeing her precious daughter being hugged by a poor boy like me I could feel her anxiety from where I sat. She glared at me as I released Clarisse and stood up.

Clarisse stood up as well, slightly shaky from her encounter with the man. "Mother, he saved me," She protested as her mother tucked her under her arm and hurried her away, cooing and tutting all the way. Hesitating, she turned to me and her eyes shined with unshed tears. "Thank you, Aleron." Clarisse whispered before she was pulled away.

I nodded, "You're welcome." My feelings sizzled beneath my skin, shame and regret...love. I didn't know what to feel anymore. Everything was spinning out of control, everyone I loved was getting hurt in some way. I didn't know what was connected and what wasn't. I was lost...so lost. I didn't know who to turn to, where to go, what questions to ask. I was tired, beyond tired. I hadn't slept much since this whole thing started and since my father had gotten hurt I had to put on a hyper awareness that took so much concentration I was exhausted every morning. I'd skipped more school and meals that I ever have had in my entire life and now my father, Alex, Clarisse, my friends... all of them were affected because of this. I was too far in to back out now, but oh how I wished. I wished I could go back to the moment I leaned against my father's door and overheard the rumors of Gustave Eiffel. I shook my head and started walking home. I'd just been standing there *thinking* after Clarisse and her mother walked into their house. On my way home, a spring shower started raining down and turning the skies gray as people all around me ran for cover. I stared up at the sky, jaw clenching as I blinked away the sky's tears that fell into my eyes. I opened my arms and tilted my head back....

I let the rain soak through my clothes, wishing it could wash me away too.

When I got home, I was soaked to the bone but it wasn't just my body that felt numb. Everything was muted to a point that the coldness that seeped into my bones from the wet clothes didn't even bother me. I walked into the parlor, my footsteps squishing as I made my way past the stunned faces of my uncle and father and sat myself down in front of the burning fire that was lit in our small fireplace.

"Aleron! You'll catch your death if you stay in those wet clothes." My father reprimanded, getting up slowly to get something to dry me off with.

"Let it happen," I mumbled under my breath, hissing when the feeling started coming back into my fingers. I apparently wasn't quiet enough.

"Aleron Aragon, do not say such a thing. Do you want your father's heart to break?" My uncle scolded me, making me feel like I was a little boy again.

The use of my first and last name sent me straight back to a day when my mother had done the same thing. I had brought in a dead pigeon and asked her if she could fix it. Now as I'm older I knew that my mother couldn't do much, but I remembered my mother trying to do what she could for an already dead bird. In the eyes of a four-year-old she was saving it. I remembered her shocked hand against her chest, "Aleron Aragon!", before crouching down and carefully taking the bird as if it was a newborn babe. I remembered her hand on my cheek, callused but soft, strong yet gentle, as she explained that the bird had already gone to heaven...my eyes misted back then as they did now, thirteen years in future. Why couldn't she be here to help me stop it, to tell me everything was going to be okay and to just *hold* me.

A warm blanket was thrown over my shoulders and I gave my father a grateful smile. He ruffled the top of my head and sat back down.

"I checked with my people at the school. As we had expected, none of them knew anything about Eiffel and the rumors." My father explained.

I listened, struggling not to shiver as life started returning to my body. I knew I should probably change into warmer clothes, but for now I stayed put and heard what he had to say.

"None of them gave me any information that wasn't more gossip or things we had already proven," My father finished, his face showing how badly he wished he could have given a better answer.

I slumped and put my head in my hands, wet strands of my hair sticking to the skin of my wrists and palms.

My uncle cleared his throat, "While your inquiries, Jacques, have brought about nothing, mine have been the opposite."

I lifted my head out of my hands, interested, but not daring to get my hopes up.

"There has been a name floating around some of the men. I asked architects, contractors, builders, mathematicians, nearly everyone who's working on the project and there was a common name that was being noticed. Émile Nouguier." He raised an eyebrow at the name, speculative. "Apparently he's a civil engineer and he worked with both Maurice Koechlin and Gustave Eiffel on the Tower."

I stood up quickly, the blanket dropping from my shoulders. "Oh, thank you Uncle François! This is *incroyable*!" I hugged him hard, his protests about getting his clothes wet falling on deaf ears. Finally, something good was coming out of this. Hopefully, this was the lead I was looking for. The name Émile Nouguier could be the one I spent all this time in search of.

***

I was surprised to receive a calling card from *Monsieur* Koechlin later that week. The messenger boy had handed it to me as I was leaving school and was gone before I could even look up from the small piece of paper.

"What is it, Al?" Asked Clarisse. She was walking back home with me. Lately we had taken to meeting up after school and walking home together.

I waved the card, the flapping noise it made making me laugh a little. "Maurice Koechlin wants me over for tea. He apparently has some information on Émile Nouguier."

Clarisse's eyes widened in surprise. I had told her who Maurice was, what he had done for me, and how he was associated with the Eiffel case. As well as the new information my uncle had found. She had also been one of the people I had helping look into who was behind the assassination plot and Eiffel's accident. Her womanly charms worked wonders.

Slipping the note in my pocket we continued our leisure walk. "Three weeks, Clarisse. I need as much help as I can get." Since my uncle had told me about Émile Nouguier, I had started looking into the name but he was a hard man to find. No one seemed to have seen him in a few months, even fewer knew where he lived. I had already checked out the few houses and addresses my uncle had managed to coerce from the people he worked with. None of them had belonged to the man named Émile.

"What do you think he's going to tell you?" Clarisse asked, her face showing her curiosity. She leaned in closer, her eyebrows furrowed.

I shrugged my shoulders. "I don't know but he wants to meet at twelve sharp. I got to get going," I bid her goodbye before heading into my house. Grabbing a satchel with paper and charcoal, just in case, I sprinted out before biking towards Maurice's address. I had to look at the paper a few times to navigate my way, and eventually I stopped in front of a beautiful cottage. The white paint and the flowers in the front made it look like something from a story book. It was much larger than my own house, this one had two stories and a huge front yard. I leaned my bike against the porch, wincing slightly at the stark contrast of the rust of the handles to the clean metal of the gate.

I patted my hair down and knocked on the door, taking off my hat as I stood there in front of the door. I felt that I looked very much out of place. As I had told Clarisse in all honesty, there was only three weeks left to find out who was behind this and stop them. I needed all the help I could possibly get.

The door opened and a lovely woman stood there, her calico green dress covered by an apron and her black hair was pulled back loosely into a bun. Her face was gentle and kind when she smiled at me.

"Aleron, welcome," She opened the door and I followed her through a large parlor into a foyer with a few chairs and large stone fireplace. "Maurice, darling. Aleron is here." That's when it clicked that this woman was Maurice's wife. It hadn't occurred to me that he might be married. I was surprised to say the least. I wondered if Eiffel was married or if he had a family.

Maurice turned from where he was looking at a piece of paper near the mantle of the fireplace, "Ah, *merci* my dear." He came over and kissed her on the cheek.

I smiled a little at their affection for one another. I hadn't had the opportunity to see many married couples.

My uncle was unmarried, and my mother had been lost when I was so young. I had no real memories of couples like this.

"I'll go make some tea, yes?" She offered, clasping her hands together near her waist. Her brown eyes crinkled at the corners as she smiled at the both of us and left.

Maurice motioned for me to take a seat as he sat down himself, his wife disappeared to make the promised tea.

"Your wife, sir?" I asked, just to be sure.

Maurice smiled, a genuine honest smile that I hadn't seen yet on his face. I had not seen any other emotion other than being stoic since I'd first met the man. "Yes, my darling Emma. Lovely, isn't she?"

I nodded, "Yes sir, she's very nice," I hesitated before my curiosity won. "Do you have any children?"

Maurice pointed to a black and white photo held in an oval frame on their mantle. The picture held Maurice, Emma and six children of different ages.

"Three boys, Pierre is the oldest, then the other two Henri, and Maurice. Three girls, Helene, Blanche, and Jeanne."

They looked like a nice family, one with many happy memories shared between them. At times, I wished I'd had a sibling or two. The children looked very proper, but happy. "You have a lovely family," I complimented him.

Emma came back with the tea, a couple of pastries on the china plate next to it. She poured us some tea and then bid us goodbye, saying she had to tend to her youngest children.

Maurice and I made idle conversation as we drank our tea and I allowed myself to eat a couple of the baked goods I rarely could afford. I filled him in on what had happened to my friend, Alex, and even the incident with Clarisse. "Honestly,

Monsieur Koechlin I need something good in my life right now, and hopefully you can give me that."

Maurice put down his teacup, the stirring spoon clicking slightly against it. He leaned back in his seat, pulling a piece of paper from his vest pocket. "Let me say this first, Aleron. You are being incredibly brave about this. I know it must be hard to do this by yourself, especially when your friends and family are getting the repercussions, but I applaud you, my boy," he handed me the folded piece of paper. "I hope this brings you some answers that you're looking for."

My chest puffed up with pride at his words. I gingerly took the paper from him, opening it. Inside was a written address of one Émile Nouguier, as well as any allegations he had with the Tower and Eiffel. This was the same name my uncle had found! This couldn't be an accident that two different people had given me the same name. I read the information, bringing it closer to my face when I read that he was seen at the construction site on the day of Alex's incident, as well as eyewitness accounts of him trailing Eiffel the days of his attack. There was even a handwriting sample on the left-hand bottom of the page. From what I could tell and remember it matched the warning note. I couldn't believe my eyes at what was just given to me. This was it! Émile Nouguier might very well be responsible for several things that had happened to me, to my family, to Eiffel.

"H-how? How do you get this?" I stammered, gesturing to the paper with one hand. "This is incredible. *C'est incroyable pour moi!"* I gushed.

Maurice gave a throaty chuckle. "I have some friends on the police force. They did a little digging for me. He seems to be the man you're looking for."

I looked down at the paper, if it was so perfect of a fit then why hadn't Maurice turned him in… *"Merci, Monsieur* Koechlin, but why haven't you told the authorities? Why not have him arrested?" My ecstasy died down some as I rationally thought about this.

"I thought you might want to be the one to do that Aleron, it seems terribly unfair if I was the one to take the man down after all of your hard work," he said as an explanation.

I thought about it for a moment, seeing his point. "Are we sure that it's him?" I questioned, doubt creeping into my voice. I looked back at the paper, I just couldn't condemn anyone that *seemed* to fit with all of the pieces.

Maurice stood up, walking across the floor and picking up his family photo. He stared at it for a moment before answering. "Take what you will from this Aleron, I believe it's the correct person, but I understand your hesitation. I'd do anything to protect my family...*will you?"*

I stared into his eyes, once again shivering a little at the lack of warmth they held. Were his words a statement or a threat? I thought about the things that this paper was condemning Émile Nouguier of. He fit some of the accusations, but some things were left unanswered. Such as why do all of this in the first place. Why would he allow himself to get seen by eyewitnesses, and the handwriting puzzled me especially...how did he even get it? Something was not right here — I was missing something. I stood up with the paper in my hands, giving it a quizzical look. I furrowed my brows as I looked at the information again. Looking Maurice in the eye, I answered his question. "Yes. I *would* do anything."

Maurice read something in my eyes as I stared at him, a test I didn't know I was taking, and nodded. "Good."

I shook his hand. "Thank you for the information *Monsieur* Koechlin, I'm looking forward to when this is all over."

Maurice smiled again and slapped my shoulder. "So am I, Aleron. So am I."

I thanked Emma for the tea as I left. I got on my bike and stared at the house for a moment. Something was wrong here I was sure of it, but what? I knew then and there that I had to talk to Émile Nouguier before doing anything else, including turning him into the authorities. I peddled off intent on meeting him.

Even if it cost me my life...after all I said I would do anything. That meant even dying for a stranger, but first I needed to meet Émile to see if he really was the person I was looking for.

✳✳✳

When I told my father that I was going to meet Émile, he wasn't altogether happy. He was hesitant like I was to meet him, but I told him that I had to know if it was true that he was the name behind the entire thing. The more I thought about it the more I thought that he wasn't. My gut screamed at me to go and see for myself before doing anything I would regret later.

My father eventually let me go and I left that same day. It was the following afternoon from when I had visited Maurice and his wife, I had wanted to talk to my father before anything, to get his advice, rather than just listening to my doubts and suspicions.

I was sitting on the steps of Clarisse's porch; I was going to ask her if she wanted to join me in meeting Émile. I had knocked on her door and received the reply that she would be there in a few minutes, that was easily thirty minutes ago. I stood up, dusting myself off from dust and went to knock again. I knocked and this time the door opened and I was met with Clarisse's face half hidden by the door, she looked frazzled.

"Aleron, today is not really a good time." She offered as an explanation.

"Are you alright?" I asked, concerned. Clarisse was not one to be shy or frazzled, seeing her this way now was unusual.

She bit her lip and looked over her shoulder, eyes worried and brow furrowed. "Aleron, please just let it be. I'm fine, just a busy day."

Before I could respond another male voice entered into the conversation, I could tell it wasn't her father or even her older brother, Paul, who was away in college outside of France.

"Clarisse, close the damn door, we are not finished talking." He ordered, voice gruff sounding. The voice got closer to the door before it was shoved open despite Clarisse's protests and I startled slightly to see the man that had harmed Clarisse just a few days ago.

"You," I growled, giving him a glare.

The man sniffed at me. "Yes, me." He looked down at Clarisse, face full of disdain. "What is the meaning of this?"

Clarisse put a hand against his chest, clearly trying to shove him backwards as she shook her head. "Please Luca, it's nothing. Aleron was just leaving," she looked at me pleadingly. "Weren't you, Al?"

I hesitated, but at her faintest of head shakes I relented. "Of course." I managed to say after a moment.

Clarisse gave me a meaningful nod and she closed the door. The man, Luca, stared at me the entire time. I couldn't believe that Clarisse's family had chosen *that* man as one of her suitors. Didn't they see that she didn't like him, that she was in fact frightened by him? I left Clarisse's house with a bitter taste in my mouth.

I shook my head and clenched my jaw as I stalked over to my bike and got on. I'd noticed I'd started going that more and more. My father noticed too, he scolded me saying I would wear down my teeth and made my jaw hurt. What he didn't know is that I needed the slight twinges of pain that traveled down my jaw because it kept me grounded, kept me focused. Maybe in a way I felt I deserved the pain.

Émile Nouguier's address was in a small neighborhood. I spent hours peddling. There were plenty of street rats in the alleys, the kids looking at me as I biked into the town. It was a dirty place. I could smell the sewers in the streets and more than one mouse passed me as I slowed my bike. I didn't think that I had much but compared to the shabby houses and the people that I passed I was as equal as the King of Spain. I suddenly felt bad at the thoughts that I had about my place in society — this neighborhood was the lowest of the low. No wonder those that looked for Émile had found it so hard, almost none of the places I passed had street names, no numbered buildings, almost nothing to identify. I went by description alone from the information that both my uncle and Maurice had given me until I came to…

I swallowed thickly at my nervousness. There was no way I could go in there, no. The address had led me to a…

maisons closes. A brothel. I looked at the large building, the lights inside illuminating men and women. The building was alive with activity, the kind I sorely didn't want to be involved with. My whole face flamed the longer I stared at it. My mother would have dragged me by the ear if she was even caught near five blocks from here. To be at its front steps was humiliating. I shook my head, "No, that's not happening." I said to myself, I got back on my bike, my foot set to push away on the peddle. I argued with myself for a moment. I had to see Émile, I had to make sure, but this….

I looked up at the top of the building, clearly the rooms and apartments part of the business below. He was in one of them, which one I didn't know, and that only angered me more. I noticed that there were some loose stones and thick vines on the side of the building leading to a window. I nodded once. "That'll do."

It did not. After I had fallen off twice and bruised both my back and ribs and after cursing the stupid vines that weren't able to hold my weight, I realized that the only option left was to go inside… I gulped loud enough that I could even hear it. I waited and bided my time, waiting for an opportunity to slip in unnoticed. Until then I walked around the building a few times, waiting to see if any back doors opened or a window left unsupervised was big enough for me to fit through. The opportunity came around dusk, a man opened the back door drunkenly, on his arm was a very busty woman. While she helped him walk away I scurried in, not unlike the rats that littered the place, and kept my head down and eyes slightly covered so I didn't see anything I didn't want to scar me for the rest of my life. Ducking down a hallway, I stuck to the wall and went mostly unnoticed until I literally ran into someone. There were several high-pitched giggles and when I looked up there were three women in front of me. Each were wearing tight corsets, with flashy and showy material as skirts and bodices.

They had no bonnets or shawls, but instead had hiked up skirts to show black stockings. Their hair, which was in various shades of brown, were styled high upon their heads with curls loose.

Their faces were aged beyond their years, eyes sad, and cheeks painted rogue.

"Well lookie here, girls. We got a young one." The darkest of the brunets laughed, her voice rough for smoking tobacco. I wanted to cover my nose from the smell of it on her clothes.

"Oh come now, Alice! He's just looking for some fun, ain't ya?" The second one said, roughly grabbing my cheek and pinching it until I felt the side of my face turn red.

Alice, apparently, laughed loudly and my face flushed even more as she pointed out how red my face was. "Well, look at the lad, all *visage rougissant* for the likes of us." she fanned her face with a fan she pulled from her corset.

"I-I, no, no you see, well I-I I'm," I stammered, trying to hide my appalled look at getting caught as well as trying very hard not to close my eyes like a little kid. I couldn't believe I was trapped between three women in a hallway and my mouth couldn't even work to say the right words.

"Poor little *môme* can't even speak right." The third one laughed and that's when I decided I'd rather the earth swallow me then entertain these women for one more second.

I cleared my throat, trying hard to sound like the seventeen-year-old man that I was and not the embarrassed boy that I was being treated like. "Excuse me please, I'm looking for someone and if you ladies-" I was cut off by the third woman giggling again.

"*Ma parole!* We've never been called ladies before." she giggled again, and I wondered if she might be drunk when she landed a predatory gaze on my face.

"Please... just let me pass." I tried to excuse myself, inching my way around them. They eventually let me pass, once I made clear that I wasn't interested in anything they were offering if it wasn't information. My face was still flushed but I was able to breathe easier once they didn't crowd me. I scurried away again, hoping that I would be able to find Émile and get out of here. I made my way up some stairs which opened to a long hall of doors. Each one looked the same mahogany brown, no numbers or anything to distinguish one from the other. I groaned at the misfortune of not knowing which one Émile was in. I prayed he didn't have company.

"Émile! Émile Nouguier!" I called out, hoping that I didn't have to knock on every door to get an answer. This area above the parlor below was definitely the living area as well as rented room. I knew this when several people, both men and women, opened their doors and yelled at me to be quiet.

I ignored them and took in a breath to yell again. "Émile Nouguier! Where are you!" Several doors slammed in anger as I yelled, but one opened at the end of the hall. A man stuck his head out and he beckoned me with his hand. I hesitantly walked over there, I didn't know if this was Émile so I kept my guard up.

"What do you think you're going?! Calling my name out for everyone to hear!" The man whispered-yelled at me. His tone was scolding and frightened at the same time. He looked to be in his mid to late thirties.

I cocked my head to the side and squinted at him. "Are you Émile Nouguier?" I asked. I looked at him and took in his rumble appearance. He *was* wearing a suit, but it was old,

99

ragged and torn. His dark black hair was combed carefully on top of his head and his black mustache accented his long nose. He had a high forehead and an angular face. His eyes darted everywhere, he looked for something, someone, but I didn't know what or who.

Before I could say anything else the man gave me a small nod and he grabbed my arm. He pulled me into the room, closing the door with a heavy slam.

"Who are you?! Answer me, *garçon*!" Émile yelled at me, pointing a slightly shaking finger in my face.

I raised my hands up in surrender. "Easy, easy," I placated. "My name is Aleron Arago."

"Who sent you?" Émile questioned, going over and closing the curtain to his window. Of course, it was the one that I was trying to get to by climbing the vine — how easy it could have been.

I shook my head, brows furrowed. "I wasn't sent by anyone. I came by myself." I put down my hands.

Émile's jaw ticked, he was clearly deciding if he believed me. He pursed his lips and shook his head. "No, *La Bête* sent you, didn't they?" Émile started panicking, taking sloppy steps backwards. "I did *everything* they asked! Now they're going to clean up, take out witnesses, aren't they? *Mon Dieu*, I'm going to die," his voice turned to a terrified whisper as he sat down on the bed that was in the middle of the room, shaking hands held to his chest. "I'm going to die."

I grew more and more confused with every word that was coming out of this man's mouth. I had no idea who he was talking about, but it did confirm that it was not Émile Nouguier that was behind the assassination. "What are you talking about?" I questioned; voice full of confusion. "I'm not here to kill you." Did he really think me, a lanky seventeen-year-old, was going to *kill* him?

"Then why are you here?!" Émile yelled. "If *La Bête* didn't send you then why are you here?" His dark eyes searched mine for an answer. He said that name with such conviction, such animosity, and fear all rolled into one. That name...could that be who I was searching for?

Chapter Eight - La Bête

*"The beast... "*I replied. "Who are they? *La Bête*?" I stood in front of Émile, there was no way I was going to sit on that bed, I caught his eye. "Are they after you? What have they told you to do?"

Émile looked up at me, face open, but gaze cautious. "You really don't know, do you?"

I shook my head. "No, I really don't," I waved my hands towards him. "Maybe you could tell me?"

He still looked suspicious, so I took in a breath and told him my story, what had happened until I had gotten here and why I was looking for him. He watched and listened with rapt attention. When I finished, he was quiet, he opened his mouth and said a few words before stopping again.

"*La Bête* is my employer," He wrung his still shaking hands. "I do not know much about him other than the fact that he pays well when I do what he asks, and that he's a man. That much I know."

I tilted my head, wanting to know more. "*La Bête* asks you to do things in exchange for money?" At his nod I asked another question. "What kind of things does he ask of you?"

Émile's lips thinned into a line and he looked down at the floor in shame. "He asked me to follow Gustave Eiffel, to cut the ropes at a construction site,"

My anger flared at that admittance. How dare he do something to my friend for something as little as money.

Émile continued, "Writing threats, making sure people got hurt or people got injured."

"Why would you do that!?" I hissed, not willing to tamper my anger. Whether this man knew or not he'd messed with my father, my friend, people I was trying to protect.

Émile startled at my tone of voice. How this man accomplished anything without acting scared I didn't know.

"*La Bête* threatened my life! I had to do what he said. He paid me well, in the beginning, but when I refused to do what he asked he threatened my life. I knew he would be good on his word too, he told me if I told anyone I would be dead before sunrise. I've seen the threads he can pull in his webs…"

"And because of this you were willing to put other people's lives in danger, to assassinate a man?" I asked, incredulously. In my mind I could see a little bit of this man's bravery at telling me all of this, even with the threat on his life, but the things he had done overruled my pity and feelings towards him.

Émile shook his head, "No! The beast had someone one else in mind for the actual assassination part."

I sighed heavily in defeat, *Mon Dieu,* there was a second person…

"Do you think you might know where *La Bête* might be found? Do you think he's in Paris? Could you describe him?" I desperately needed some type of information, something, anything.

Again, the man in front of me shook his head, I was beginning to wonder what help he was at all. "No, we only met once face to face when he first hired me and even then he was in the shadows." He thought before answering my other question. "I don't think he's in Paris, from what I knew he was from Veytaux, Switzerland."

My eyes went wide at that, "Switzerland?! And he has control in Paris, France?" I closed my eyes, soaking in the damning information. How was I ever going to stop the man behind it all if he was in *Switzerland*?

"What was supposed to happen after that? After you did what he asked?" I ended up saying after a while of silence.

"He would let me go, pay me handsomely. All I was to be was merely the one that was going to take the blame. I was not to be found; I was to disappear forever." Émile paused. "In fact, how *did* you find me?"

I opened my mouth to answer when the sound of shattering glass and a choked yell cut me off.I hit the floor with a thump, my elbows bruising at the impact as I covered my head. Émile hit the floor as well on the other side of the bed, a second shot rang out like a thunderbolt inside the room. More glass rained down on me, I was directly underneath the window.

"Mon Dieu!" I breathed out in shock. Someone was shooting at us! My chest heaved as I breathed harshly onto the floorboards, the screams of the women below and in the other rooms loud enough to be heard through the walls. The yelling of men was deeper, more distinct. Glass cut into my hands and torso as I crawled over to the other side of the bed, my breath catching in my throat.

Émile was laying on his back, a hand against the blooming red flower on his chest, a pool of that hated liquid already underneath him. His face was pale and breathing shallow.

I panicked a little, what did I do? Was he dying? Could I call for help? How do you treat a bullet wound? What do I do? *What do I do?*

I lifted myself up on my elbows, crouching slightly over Émile's body, his pained eyes looking into mine.

"I'm going to help, I'm going to try." I told him, panicked breaths that I was barely able to conceal escaped my mouth. I crouched, looking out the broken window, the sharp shards still standing catching the barely rising sun. I let out a shuddered breath. Émile's words whispered coldly in my head, *'he told me if I told anyone I would be dead before sunrise.'* There didn't seem to be any more shots coming through, so I grabbed the sheets that were on the bed and pressed them to the wound that was seeping blood onto Émile's chest.

Émile's bloody hands clamped over my wrist as I pressed on the wound, trying to stem the blood flow. The metallic smell that I hated was starting to permeate the air and the thickness, the warmth of his blood started soaking through the cloth. The man coughed and blood bubbled into his mouth. He met my eyes with the same resolved look I knew he read in mine. We both knew he was dying.

I shook my head. "No, I'm sorry. This is my fault." I pulled back the cloth and quickly saw the bullet hole fill again. I nearly gagged but managed to hold it in. "I'm sorry," I whispered, watching Émile's skin turn shades whiter.

"I-I t-tol-ld you, A-l-leron." Émile whispered with a terrible smile filled with crimson. I knew that his earlier words would be coming true. Already his grip on my wrist was starting to slacken. "Y-y-ou.." He paused and groaned as pain shot through his chest. The cloth I was holding was mostly red now. He took in a ragged, gurgled breath and tried speaking again. "Can't e-e-sscape him."

"Who's him?" I hated asking a dying man for his last words to be an answer to my question, but it was so needed, desperately needed. He had to know something. "Please Émile, who is *he*?" Oh God, what had I done? I'd killed this man as sure as if I had pulled the trigger myself. I pulled him out of hiding, I coerced him to answer, persuaded him to give information, oh...oh no... I did this...

Émile swallowed thickly, blood running down his chin. He tried to say something, but couldn't. I learned down closer to hear him and he tried valiantly to speak again.

"R-reesse." He slurred.

I pulled back, giving him a questioning look. "Reese?"

Émile shook his head, opened his mouth and his last breath left his mouth instead of words. His life left his eyes as we kept eye contact, turning them into a marbled brown. He stared blankly at me. I'd never seen a dead person's eyes before... With my mother her eyes were closed. I gave Émile the same courtesy, I closed his eyes with a brush of my hands, his skin still warm. I slumped back against the bed, hands shaking so badly I thought they were matching my beating heart. I shivered violently, putting my hands up to cover my mouth before I noticed they were covered in someone else's blood. They were stained with scarlet that I'd never intended to be there.

"Holy…" I started, still staring at Émile who was ever so still on the floor in front of me, never going to move again. *"Mon Dieu…"* I shakily stood up on legs that I didn't think would hold me and just made it to the washing bowl when I heaved everything I had in me. I gagged as tears ran down my face, whether from guilt or the force of my stomach's clenching I didn't know.

Once that stopped, I was able to take a few deep breaths. I rubbed my cheeks, forgetting about the blood covering my hands until I saw the red streaks on my face in the looking glass. Who was this Reese? Émile's last word had been that name… Reese. Who was he? What does he have against Eiffel? Why bother with France when he's in Switzerland? I had so many questions, my head spun, looking for which way was up.

"I have to get out of here," I told myself, trying to pull back some of that resolve and anger I had in the beginning of this visit, anything to hide behind. If anyone found me with a dead body… I stumbled as I walked, my train of thought made me shake a little. "Émile's dead…" I said out loud, looking back into the mirror as I left the room. "And it's your fault." I told him — my reflection — my face looked back at me…I couldn't read it.

I hurried out of the room, drowning in the panic that was still surrounding everyone and everything downstairs and even in the hall. Several doors were left open to rooms, women crying, and men drinking. I saw an officer or two and I ran the opposite direction. The police were the last thing I needed right now, the last thing I needed was from one of them to recognize me. The sun was barely rising as I ran out the back door, nearly as fast as I had first ran in. At the moment I couldn't even think of a sun rise without hearing Émile's words echo through my ears. I ran and ran, tears blurring my vision, my chest and leg's burning… I'd ran for at least a mile or two before I remembered the bike I had left behind. In my haste to leave I had left it in front of the brothel, leaning against the vines that I'd tried to climb. I bent over my knees, breathing harsh in the quiet morning. It was the time between the moon disappearing and the sun barely rising when everything was still asleep, so still, so quiet you could hear the wind. I yelled into the quietness so fiercely a flock of birds flew up from a tree. I gripped my hair with blood cracking fingers and stumbled, choking on sobs. Falling to my knees I cried, yelling into the dirt with a tear clogged throat. "Why me?!" I shouted. "Why did it have to be me?" I cursed my own curiosity, my own heart, my pity, my righteous anger. Why did I become attached, why did I investigate? What good does having a big heart do if it breaks all the time? *Why...why...why?*

I managed to pull myself up after some time — numb once again — I set off walking. It would take me a few hours to make it home, I rubbed my forehead, my father would probably be so worried. Most of the walk home was blurry, I don't remember much of it, by the time I was standing in my neighborhood I blinked sluggishly. I didn't remember how I'd gotten here, or where my feet were taking me. I made it to Clarisse's door, just noticing that it was her door when my hand knocked softly. It was still early morning, what was I doing? I wasn't thinking straight.

I shook my head and turned to walk back down her steps when my legs gave out and I sank heavily onto the steps.

"Aleron?" A soft voice asked, her voice pouring over me like a balm to the ache I held in my chest.

I turned when a hand went against my cheek, bringing me face to face to an extremely concerned Clarisse. "What happened? Whose blood is this?" Her gaze flitted over my face, taking in the blood, the ragged appearance and the bags that were no doubt under my eyes.

I shook my head. I couldn't answer at the moment.

She nodded, understanding, somehow. Her eyes said all I needed to know.

"Help," I pleaded, gripping her wrist like Émile did to mine only a few hours ago. "I can't do this." I let out a sob, "I'm sorry." I broke down.

Clarisse tucked me under her chin, wrapping her arms around my shoulders. "Shh, I'm here, you're okay." She whispered.

I tightened my hand against her wrist, sobbing against her chest. I felt a featherlight kiss land against my hair. I didn't want to think about what I'd seen tonight, what I'd witnessed. What I'd *caused*. I stuttered and told her what had happened to Émile, what happened before, and how he died.

Clarisse held me close, rocking us side to side as I managed to calm down enough to try and restore some of my masculinity.

I wanted to thank her, for holding me; for sticking with me; for helping me. I wanted to tell her was special she was to me, I wanted to just be with her...I wanted to tell her I loved her. "Clarisse, I-" I stopped when I noticed something catching the early sunlight on her hand.

I pulled away from her a little, picking up her hand and tapping the silver band on her left ring finger. "What's...what's this?" I dared to ask, my voice broken and hoarse.

Clarisse didn't look me in the eye when she took her hand back, placing it in her lap. "Luca asked for my hand in marriage....my parents said yes." She spun the band on her finger. "We're engaged now, betrothed." She looked down at the floor, her locks of hair covering her face. "The wedding is set later this year."

My heart broke into a million pieces, the shards piercing my lungs, my chest. For a moment I couldn't breathe, couldn't live. "Oh..." I got out, voice breaking on that one word. "Congratulations." I managed, pulling all the way away from her until there was space between us. That ache in my heart grew with this added news, my mind supplied that I was too late to make my feelings known. She was betrothed. Clarisse was getting married — I'd lost one of the few good things I had in my life right now. I cleared my throat and squeezed my hands together, more of the dried blood flaking off. "Clarisse..." I started, turning to her.

Her mouth was on mine before I could even think of another word. I was stunned at what she was doing, she was kissing *me*. Clarisse Alix was kissing Aleron Arago. Hurriedly I cupped her cheek and kissed her back, responding to it before it was gone.

Clarisse pulled back slowly, both of us panting slightly at the unexpected turn of events. Her blue eyes seemed to look into my soul as she kissed me again, softly, just once. "*Pardonne moi*," She breathed out, her eyes looking into mine, her perfect face tilting up a little at this angle with our close proximity.

I looked at her, wondering why she was apologizing, but still reeling that she'd kissed me. *Did* Clarisse love me? Did she care for me like I did her? Could it be true? I took her hands in mine, clenching them tightly. "Clarisse?" I asked in question...looking into her face but she looked down from my gaze. No.

"I have to go Aleron," She said suddenly, taking her hands out of mind. "I'm sorry." I heard her breath catch as she stood up and ran back up her steps. She looked back at me and regret was clear on her face. "I'm sorry." She whispered again. I looked down at the floor, biting my lip as I knew she regretted kissing me.

I stood up and walked backwards away from her. "It's all right Clarisse." I told her, my resolve faltering with every step and word that left my mouth. "Everyone has to go sometimes…" I shook my head sadly. "I can never trust anyone to stay." I turned away from her before she could see my face crumple, my lips trembling, and my hands still shaking. I'm sure she already saw the slumped shoulders, my head looking down. I turned around and didn't look back, but oh how I wanted to. This investigation had nearly cost me my father, but now it had cost me Clarisse. I was just too blind to see what was right in front of me. I hated myself for it. I walked home as numb as the day my mother died.

I opened my door to find my father there in front of me. His usually stern face melted into concern as he took in my appearance. I slumped into his chest, slouching until my forehead leaned against his collar bone. My father didn't say anything but just wrapped his arms around me.

He herded me into my room, cleaned my hands and face, and settled me down on my bed.

"Get a couple of hours of rest, Al." He told me, kissing the top of my head. "Then we can talk."

I didn't answer and stayed awake in my bed, watching the sun rise further and further into the sky from my window. Every time I blinked I saw Émile's prone form on the floor, my hands stained red. Eventually after a few hours of just staring at my ceiling I got up, changed into clean blood free clothes, and met my father in the parlor. He had food for me, a few slices of bread and some cheese. I nibbled on it while he stared at me.

"What happened Al?" He asked after a few moments of silence.

"I visited Émile," I offered as an explanation. "And it cost him his life." I said, my voice monotone and emotionless. I looked up at my father. "He was shot for trying to tell me things about the assassination. All I learned was a name, well two. *La Bête,* the beast,and Reese."

"*La Bête?"* He asked, with a raised eyebrow.

I nodded solemnly. "Here's what I know…" and I told him what Émile had told me. I told him about the gunshot, Émile's death, where I had found him. Who *La Bête* was and the supposed name of the man, Reese, that was behind this entire plot.

Afterwards we stayed silent for a moment, the bread that I had eaten swirling in my stomach as I retold trying to save Émile Nouguier — the man who'd been blackmailed into the assassination — the man I caused to die.

"I don't think I've ever heard of anyone with that name." My father told me, a hand against his chin in thought.

I shook my head. "I wouldn't think so, supposedly he lives in Switzerland. He has ties here and a strong enough vengeance against Eiffel that it has traveled continents."

My father gave me a look like he thought I was joking but when I didn't say anything else he sighed in truthful remorse. "I'm so sorry Aleron, I can't believe you saw something like that." He looked at me sorrowfully, placing a comforting hand on my shoulder. "What do you want to do?"

"What can I do?" I answered him, "Other than keep carrying on." I groaned and put my face into my hands, rubbing my eyes until I saw white spots. "There's two weeks until the deadline. Two *weeks, père*. That's all that's left." I sighed deeply, feeling helplessness try to settle in my bones, I shivered trying to dislodge it. "He's playing a game with me, a waiting game. I just have to keep going, keep trying to figure out who this Reese is."

My father nodded, seeing the struggle on my face. "I'm sure I could ask your uncle if he's ever heard of the name. I'll ask some people I know."

I chuckled mirthlessly. "Father, if your people didn't know who Émile was I doubt very much that they'll know who an unknown man in Switzerland is."

My father gave a small laugh. "Very true Al, very true." He took away my barely eaten food and left me to my thoughts.

I knew that my father saw that I was hiding something from him, but I didn't want to tell him about my mishap with Clarisse. I was too embarrassed to even think more than a second on it again. For now, I could escape my parent's intuition, but I knew he'd ask sooner or later. For now, I had bigger things to think about like finding out more information on this man from Switzerland. I didn't know where to start, but what I did know is what I told my father. I'd just have to keep going. I left shortly after that; my father tried to make me rest some more but I brushed him off. I had work to do and little time to do it.

112

I went to Alex's shop, his apartment was above it. The stairs in the back led me to it's front door, also green, just like the shop below. It was dead and empty, closed until Alex was able to fully recover. He'd been moved from the doctor's to his own house a few days ago. The infection had thankfully settled with medicine and lots of prayer. Alex had lost his leg from the fall, but had managed to keep the other from infection. His chest was still sore and some of his ribs still unstable, but he was still fighting to stay alive and for that I was thankful. His niece from Bordeaux had come to take care of him, she was near my age, a little older, but still younger than Alex. I had met her a few times, once when she'd come to Paris with her husband to visit Alex and another when I'd traveled through Bordeaux when my mother was ill. She was a kind soul, a gentle touch of caring hands. I knocked on the door and stuck my hands in my pockets, waiting for an answer.

The door opened and much to my surprise, Alex was standing there. More like leaning as he stood on wood crutches. His face was still tight with pain, but he was smiling. He looked better than he was in the doctor's room, but he was still pale, skinner, and his eyes looked tired. Alex's leg was still wrapped in white bandages, his dark green pant leg cuffed up a few inches above it.

"Que faites-vous!" I scolded with a smile as I steadied my friend as he reached out a hand to touch my shoulder. "Should you even be standing? Laying down?"

"Can't do anything that way," Alex chuckled, giving my shoulder a firm squeeze. "It's good to see you my friend."

I helped Alex to a chair at his table, leaning his crutches against it. "It's good to see you too Alex, how are you feeling?" I fixed both Alex and I with a cup of tea to busy my hands. "I thought your niece was taking care of you?" I looked at him questionably.

113

Alex waved a hand at my question about his health, skipping it. "She is, she's wonderful. An emergency at home called her away for a few days, she'll be back by tomorrow." He groaned slightly as he shifted on his chair, pulling his tea closer. "I can manage for a day or two by myself."

"Can you?" I joked, just realizing he didn't have his glasses on his face and was squinting into his tea. "Where are your glasses?"

"By the table," Alex said, taking a sip. "I haven't had a chance to fix them, me being held up in bed and all."

I stood up and grabbed them, looking them over. Luckily the glass parts weren't cracked or scratched more than normal. The arm of his glasses were bent and its hinges were missing a part. "Alex, I can fix these. Easily." I took them over and made some room on his small table, pushing my tea away. I wasn't that hungry anyway. I went and grabbed his tool kit from his cupboard, I know my way around Alex's house from the many times he'd invited me over to talk and tea after working my hours at the apprenticeship.

"Thank you, Al. I appreciate that. My hands have not been too steady lately." Alex admitted, showing me his slightly shaking hand.

I ducked my head in embarrassment, "I'm so sorry Alex. If I had gotten there faster…" I trailed off, clicking my jaw together.

"Hey now," Alex reprimanded. "Don't do that to yourself." He patted my hand as I picked up a tool. "If you hadn't gotten there, I would've been a dead man."

I flinched slightly at his words. He didn't know how true that statement really was. "Well…" I cleared my throat. "I'm just glad I made it." I ended up saying.

Alex filled me in on how he was feeling while I fixed his glasses, simply straightening the arm and replacing the part that was missing. I cleaned his lenses and handed them to him.

"I'm glad you're feeling better Alex, you're having a very positive outlook on it all."

Alex put on his glasses, blinking his eyes for a moment and then smiled. "Aleron, I think missing a leg is much better than dying. I would rather I have both, but it's not as bad as it could have been." He paused. "The doctors said that I was damn lucky to have made it past the infection, it nearly turned sepsis. There's still some healing left to go, feeling phantom pains in a limb that's not there, but Al... I'm alive and that's all that matters. "He held up a finger, "Here is the bottom line. *Qui n'avance pas, recule.* Do you know what that means?"

I shook my head, "No, I'm not really getting your point."

Alex laughed a little. "*Qui n'avance pas, recule.* One who does not move forward, recedes." He raised an eyebrow and titled his head. "Now I have two choices, I can either mope and belittle myself for only having one leg and let it hinder my life, or I can move forward. Accept it as it becomes part of my life, accept the consequences, the challenges, and move on. If I stand still, I will move backwards." He nodded at me, focusing on my face. "Understand now?"

I did. I felt like Alex was talking not only about his leg, but to me. He didn't know about the Gustave Eiffel investigation I was doing, but somehow his words helped. I had to accept the consequences, face the challenging moments and move on. If I was going to accomplish anything to save Eiffel I had to move on. I smiled for the first time in a while and stood up. "*Merci,* thank you!" I hugged him carefully and quickly, "You just gave me the answer I was looking for." I hurried out of the room, "Thank you Alex!" I yelled back up as I thundered down the stairs. Alex's surprised, confused, but cheerful laugh following me as I burst out of the shop. Going at a run I headed to the library, then after that I went to the police station asking for any information on Reese. There wasn't much. other than a few nobody troublemakers under the name, none from Switzerland. After that I went to the telegram office and asked around for anything from Switzerland or the name again. I left there empty handed, but my spirits were still high. My father's people knew next to nothing, same with my uncle's. There was still one more place I could go. Back to the man himself. Gustave Eiffel.

***

I knocked frantically on his door, my chest heaving from the run I had made. I was going to have the strongest legs of the boys my age by the time this whole thing was over, with all this running around. I was also feeling slightly dizzy from having not eaten anything in a while. The door opened to a startled Gustave, looking much healthier and the sling was gone from the last time I had seen him. It'd been weeks.

"Do you know anyone from Switzerland?" I asked once he'd let me inside, giving him no pause.

Eiffel thought, his bushy eyebrows furrowing down. "No...I do not think I do. Why?"

"I think I might have a new lead, *Monsieur*. I met a man named..." I thought aboutÉmile Nouguier and his death and it sent a spike of regret through me. "Never mind that, I met someone who gave me the name Reese, at least that's what I believe to be the name." I looked away as I remembered that

Émile had shaken his head when I asked if it was the right name, but...it was all I had. "I was told he might be from Switzerland." Shrugging my shoulder and raising my hands a little I said, "This might be the man we've been looking for. Who might be after you."

"*C'est incroyable!*" Eiffel said, excitement and relief flooding his face.

I couldn't correct him by telling him it was just a guess, just a speculation. His crestfallen face caught my attention again.

"*Je suis désolé*, Al." Gustave apologized, genuinely looking terribly distraught. "I don't know of anyone who lives or lived in Switzerland, there is no one by the name of Resse first or last that I know. No friend, no apprentice, no family. There's not even a project crew member that has had that name as far as I can remember."

I hung my head. "*Merde*," I said softly under my breath. "That leaves me nowhere."

"Perhaps..." Eiffel startled, taking his chin. "Yes, perhaps *Monsieur* Koechlin could help you. He has a few friends on the police force. I'm sure he would be willing to help if you asked."

I bit my lip and nodded. While I was hesitant to ask for outside help, *Monsieur* Koechlin did know about the invitation I was holding for his friend. He even gave me the information about Émile without my asking because he knew I was looking into it. He might be of some use. "I think I'll go see him now." I offered my thanks to Eiffel and left. It was around dinner time now but if I paid a coach to drop me off I could make it there and back by nightfall. I kept forgetting that I'd left my bike near the brothel, someone else probably had stolen it by now. Curse my foolishness. I persuaded a coach and its driver to drop me off for a *france* which was what I spent an entire week working for as an apprentice, but it was worth it in the long haul. I jumped down and thanked the man as he drove off before I walked up the steps to that beautiful cottage again.

I hit the door with the knocker a few times, the blackbird on the handle made great thumps that echoed into the house. I bit my lip in thought as I paced a little outside the door in anticipation.

Monsieur Koechlin opened the door, the smile he had on his face sliding off as he saw me darkening his doorway. I could hear his family in the background. He sighed. "There goes my dinnertime." He gripped his cloth napkin in his hand as he opened the door a little further. "Come in, Aleron."

"*Pardonne-moi* for interrupting, but I need your help." I told him, taking off my hat that I had grabbed from my room earlier this morning and wringing it in my hands.

"Let's go into my study, there we can talk." Maurice offered, waving a hand towards the door.

I thanked him and sat down. "I think I know who's behind this." I explained the moment he closed the door.

"Behind the assassination?" Maurice asked in surprise, raising an eyebrow.

I nodded. "Yes, but I need your help to be sure." I told him then about Émile, what happened with the shooting, what he had told me as he was dying, the tip about Switzerland and the name Reese.

Monsieur Koechlin pinched the bridge of his nose. "Oh Aleron, Aleron." He sighed and stood up. "He was supposed to keep quiet," He mumbled under his breath. Maurice went to the mantel, looking again at his family picture. "I was hoping you wouldn't find out."

I grew confused. "What?" I questioned. "Find out what?" I was growing more and more concerned as I watched Maurice's eyes turn stone cold as he looked at me. Like a snake's. A devil's. My eyes widened in shock. "*Mon Dieu*, it's you!" I whispered, stunned beyond belief. Panic settled in as I realized that Émile wasn't trying to say Reese, but *Maurice*.

Maurice gave a small bow and nodded, "You were supposed to die right along with Émile Nouguier. There were two shots, a shame that both didn't hit their targets."

My brain didn't communicate with my body fast enough as I tried to register just what he was saying. Oh God, Maurice Koechlin was behind all of it, he knew about the plot and about my infestation because I *told* him. He knew where I was going, my family, my loved ones because I had *told* him. How had he known every step I was going to take, had made? I scrambled out of my chair and went to open the door. I skidded to a stop when I was met with two burly men. One was skinnier but tall and evil looking. The other was larger and just to show me that he cracked his knuckles.

"Surprised, no?" Maurice asked me, as I spun back to him, a wicked grin on his face. "I had hoped that you'd been taken care of at the same time as that incompetent Émile, but...here we are."

"You...you...Eiffel is your friend!" I stuttered. I was trapped between the three men, the burlier two blocking my only exit. "How could you do that?"

Maurice tutted, "I have no need to explain myself to you, Al."

Anger flooded my system, the red ball that I'd been holding exploding in my chest. "How dare you!?" I yelled, barely noticing when the two bodyguards, if you could call them that, gripped my arms. I kicked at them, straining to get to Koechlin.

"You *bastard*! My father, Émile, Alex, Eiffel! It was all you!" I snarled at him.

Maurice shook a finger at me, "No, no, no, not *just* me." He turned to the taller of the two brutes that were holding me. "Jon, could you please go get our special guest?"

I shivered at the look he gave me as the man left. Soon I heard shouting, a woman's voice, and soon yelling. My heart sunk in my chest to the pit of my stomach as my head drooped. I knew those yells; I knew that voice.

I closed my eyes as Luca brought Clarisse into the room, the other man following behind.

Luca had an iron grip on her forearm, while Clarisse struggled against him. Catching sight of me she stilled. Her terrified gaze met mine, her blue eyes wide and fearful.

I shook my head and stopped struggling, looking pleadingly at Maurice. "Don't hurt her, don't." My voice cracked against my will. "She's innocent, she doesn't know anything."

Maurice's laugh startled me. "*Innocent?*" He questioned, he took a step closer to Clarisse, running a finger down her cheek as she gave him a disgusted look. "No, she is not innocent. Meet my partner."

I looked between him and Clarisse. "What?" I didn't believe it, I wouldn't. "Clarisse, what is he talking about?!"

Clarisse started crying, staying silent.

"Oh, now that pretty mouth of yours is closed." Maurice taunted. He turned towards me. "Clarisse here has been a beautiful little informant. Luca made sure to keep her in line, and of course with her father in my debt: drugs, drink, money. She didn't have much of a choice but to follow my orders." He shook his head. "If you had just left things be you might have been able to be with her Aleron." He clapped his hands together once. "*Ç'est ce que ç'est.*" He shrugged.

Clarisse only cried harder. "I'm sorry, I'm so sorry." She pleaded, a hand covering her mouth.

I clenched my jaw and looked down, no words could describe what I felt at that moment. Every time I had confided in Clarisse, she had told everything to Maurice, to Luca. Every time I told her when I was going, what steps I was taking in the investigation, my suspects, all of it... Everything was told to Maurice. I knew right then that it was true. I remembered all of the times I had told Clarisse what was going on, then shortly after a disaster happened. My father... Alex's accident...the threatening notes... the stolen box...Émile's death...

All of it was because of Clarisse. I couldn't look at her, yet even now her sobbing tore at my heartstrings.

I sniffed to hide the tears that threatened to overcome me. "I hate you." I didn't know who I was talking to, Maurice or Clarisse.

The door to Koechlin's study opened and a young boy came in, unphased by the people being held hostage or the brutish men in his father's study.

"*Père,* mama says to come finish dinner." He said as Maurice picked him up.

"Of course, Henri." Maurice said, smiling to his son.

I gaped I couldn't understand how this man could be a father to his children yet at the same time this hateful and vengeance filled man. The longer I stared at the boy the more I thought I'd seen him before. It struck me in between the eyes when I realized that this was the same young boy that had given me the first threatening note. If that wasn't clue to everything leading towards Maurice Koechlin as the man behind Gustave Eiffel's assassination, I didn't know what would be.

"Why?" I asked, voice wavering just slightly. I was terrified, but I was trying not to show it. "How?" I asked instead.

Maurice put down his son. "Clarisse, and the fact that most of Paris's police department is in debt. Money, women, illegal goods all come for a price. Same with Clarisse's father, his debt earned his daughter into my service as spy. Luca will take good care of her, don't worry about that, Aleron. As for Switzerland... I was born in Switzerland, Veytaux specifically. Not many know about that. You're privileged, Al." He tsked his tongue. "As for why...well I guess you'll never find out will you?" Flicking his hand to the hallway he added, "Jon, Luca, Victor, please take these two to the basement. We'll deal with them when dinner is finished. Emma made duck. *Merci.*"

He thanked them as if it was a daily occurrence and I felt the blood drain away from my face a little as I realized that it might very well be. I don't have any time to think when something was slammed into the back of my head and the floor raised up to meet me as everything went black.

***

I woke up groggily, my head was throbbing and something sticky was running down my face. I groaned softly, trying to access the damage. Moving my legs, I felt they were fine, nothing broken, and no ankles sprained. Moving up I took in a few breaths and didn't feel anything pull. Good, nothing broken. I tried moving my arms and strained against something. Looking as best I could over my shoulder. I saw I was tied at the wrists around a sturdy pole, I moved my wrists and felt them chafe against the thick rope. As I grew more conscious, I started hearing sniffling.

"Clarisse?" I groaned, my head throbbing more as I spoke. I'm not sure if I yelled or whispered her name, but she heard me all the same.

"Aleron!" She yelled, voice hitching.

I hissed, "Don't yell." I moved my arms again, my fingers running along the rope tied around the pole, I felt another pair of wrists and realized that Clarisse and I were tied together, back to back, and pole in between us. I could hear her crying and I was surprised that I didn't feel pity or sadness for her years, it made me angry. I cared for this woman so much and she'd betrayed me. Betrayed my family, my friends. An innocent man. For now, I had to shove those feelings away and focus on getting out of here. "Where are we?" I demanded, trying to look around the dark room. It was pitch black in there, when I came to I wasn't sure my eyes were open. The dirt was cold underneath me, but the walls felt like wood where I could brush my leg against them. I wondered if the pole I was tied to was a support beam.

Clarisse sniffled, "We're in *Monsieur* Koechlin's basement. It's where he holds people."

I bristled, in anger, in spite, in defeat. "Great, just bloody great." I growled out, the war drums in my head not receding. We lapsed back into silence, just waiting for when Maurice finished his dinner to do what he willed with us. I leaned my head against the pole, exhaustion suddenly pulling at my eyelids.

"Aleron?" Clarisse asked, hesitantly.

"Hmm?" I could feel her pull the ropes to shift, trying to see me.

"I'm so sorry Al," She started.

I didn't want to hear it, I really didn't, but at the same time I *did* want to know why. To hear her explanation, to hear if...maybe she still did love me. Was that all a game, was it all a plot? Was she always connected to Maurice and his family ties or did she get wrapped into it by her father like Koechlin had said? I didn't know what to think, who to believe. That seemed to be a common feeling I've had in the last few weeks, since this whole thing started. I let her continue.

"I didn't have a choice, Aleron." She explained.

I hmphed, people always had a choice, it might be a hard one but there was always a choice. "Why not?" I asked, closing my eyes.

"My father...he got into Maurice's debt. Gambling, stolen goods, women... he owed him so much..." Clarisse gulped down a sob. "Maurice made him give up his only daughter to even the debt. I tried fighting, but then Maurice brought in Luca and he was always there, always making sure I was spying on your father, on you."

I clenched my jaw, listening to her story.

"I don't want to marry him Al," She let loose a whimper and it still tore at my heart.

"Then don't." I told her, "Run to Paul, he's your brother and in college. You didn't have to stay here Clarisse, I didn't know anything about this, no one did. You could have vanished and I still would have cared for you."

She protested, "How could I?! He would've killed my father!"

"And mine could've been!" I yelled back at her, turning around trying to see her. It was pointless, I couldn't see anything, but I could feel her stunned silence. She'd seen my anger before, towards bullies, Val, Tomas, but never her. Never Clarisse. I swallowed thickly, trying to temper back the emotions I was feeling. "My father didn't count Clarisse? My friend, Alex? He didn't count?"

She was quiet.

I took that as her answer, I left her in silence for a while, my heart dying to know a certain question's answer before I didn't have a chance. "Why? Why did you spy on me? Why did you use me?" My heart sunk to my stomach as I remembered the blue piece of fabric. "The letters...in my room...all that paper and proof. You destroyed it didn't you?" I asked, voice barely above a murmur.

Clarisse sniffed, "My dress ripped...I did not realize till it was too late."

I shook my head, trying to hold in the exasperated scoff that was building in the back of my throat. "Don't you have any remorse for the people you helped Maurice hurt? For what you did to them? To *me*?" My voice broke a little on the last word, my emotions coming to a breaking point.

"I had to..."

"Well that's not good enough Clarisse!" I shouted. "People will die, people *have* died!" My mind went back to Émile's murder. "I thought you were my friend," I looked back at her, emotions making my voice shake as I leaned my head back against the pole. "I loved you Clarisse, *zut*, I still love you Clarisse." I whispered.

125

"I did what I had to Aleron," She said eventually. "I-I thought I would have a second chance, a redo, fix the things I did-"

"This isn't a game, Clarisse! This is real life, people get hurt when we make mistakes, there are no do overs, nothing to fix. You don't get to redo some things when you make a choice!" I flexed in the ropes, trying to loosen them, making my wrists ache and turn raw as I got flooded with regret.

"I told you everything! I trusted you! You used it all against me, all of it!" I gave up with a huff, the ropes now slightly slick with blood from my struggle.

Clarisse was silent behind me, her sniffling gone. "I regret.....I regret all of it. Me...my choices...my father's choices...Maurice...*you*."

I blew out a breath, my heart sinking and making my stomach hurt from her rejection. I thought that maybe she loved me, now I wondered if it all was an act. If somehow, she knew Luca or Maurice's people were watching and she had to get to me.

"Was any..." I took in a strengthening breath. "Was *any* of it real?" I asked, my voice so low it felt like a rumbled sound.

"......yes." She admitted after a moment's pause, she drew in a shuddering breath and then remained silent. She gave me no further information.

I felt numb again, felt sick to my stomach, lightheaded, exhausted. "*Merci,* Clarisse." I let out a sarcastic chuckle. "Thank you for regretting me, I'm sure I was useful."

Clarisse gave a scoff-ish sound. "Aleron, please, don't be petty."

"Petty?" I asked, astounded. I nodded my head a few times. "Is that how you see it?"

"I left clues, I helped when I could Al! I wasn't just working for Maurice." She protested, her voice no longer having tears in it.

My mind thought back to the last weeks, the things that happened. I sighed. "It was you who sent the telegram to my uncle didn't you?"

"I did," Clarisse admitted, "I-I didn't-I didn't want this to happen Aleron. *Mon Dieu* if I had known it was going to get this big... If I had known you were going to investigate...If I had known that Maurice had my father in his debts....there would be so much that I would change."

"*C'est la vie, mon chéri.*" I told her, "That is life... If we knew all of it...there would be a lot that we would all change." My mother, my eavesdropping, my feelings for Clarisse, the Eiffel Tower.

We were silent afterwards. My best friend, my closest friend I confided in, my *belle* Clarisse had betrayed me. Had stolen from me, endangered those I loved, spied on me, and had helped a terrible man. Now we were both waiting for the consequences. One of choice, the other of coincidence. I didn't know how long we waited, how much time passed, what Maurice was going to do to us. If my father noticed that I hadn't returned home, I cursed myself when I realized what I hadn't even told him where I was going, who I was seeing. I slumped against my bonds, there wasn't any help coming. We were trapped in a basement and Eiffel was still in danger. *I* was in danger now. Did I fail?

The door banged open with a loud thunk as it hit the opposite wall. I squinted against the bright light as Clarisse and I stared up at the *voyou*that was standing at the top step. Two men came down the stairs, Luca and the other one Jon. They came and grabbed me, pulling me away from Clarisse and the basement. I struggled against them, yelling and kicking. I heard Clarisse scream when I got punched in the gut, pain spiked in my entire body from the force of Luca's punch and I went down to my knees. I curled around my stomach, trying to breath as they retied my wrists behind me.

"Aleron!" Clarisse screamed for me, as I was shoved and pulled up the stairs.

"Clarisse!" I called back, kicking and bucking like a wild horse trying to break free.

"Aler-"

Her call was cut off by the basement door slamming shut, she was still down there, tied up. I was...I didn't know where I was going or what was going to happen. From the looks of Jon and Luca I didn't think they were going to be good. I was taken through the back of the house, any sign of Koechlin's family — Emma, Henri, Pierre, all of the kids — were gone. It was still and eerily quiet. I shivered a little at the chill that ran down my spine. I was shoved through the kitchen, also devoid of cook or staff, and thrown roughly to the dirt once we were out the back door. I lifted my head and saw there was a small wall behind the house, leading towards a neighbor's backyard, there were dozens of trees, thick oaks that made me think of Val, Tomas, Clarisse, and I's special spot in the park near my house. It filled me with a sense of calmness, of acceptance, and of peace. I picked myself up off the floor, grass stains on my pants. Luca came next to me and cut off the ropes that dug into my wrists.

I jerked back once he was done and eyed him suspiciously. "You're letting me go?" I rubbed my bloody wrists, hissing. "Why?"

Luca chuckled sadistically. "We're not letting you go, *imbécile.*" He pulled out a revolver, making me watch as he put bullets into the gun. He spun the cylinder and clicked it shut. "We're letting the rabbit run."

I eyed him wearily, the gun making my veins turn to ice.

He chuckled again. "Oh you didn't know? It's hunting season." He pointed the gun at me.

I took off, all that running came in handy now. I ran in a zig, zag, hoping that would throw off his aim. Holy… it suddenly dawned on me that someone was going to shoot me! I stumbled when I hit a dip, my own thoughts distracting me. *Merde sainte!* I threw my arms over my head as I heard a bullet struck a tree near me.

"Come on now! Make this a little hard." Luca taunted from behind me, his voice echoing.

I wondered suddenly if Jon had a gun too, oh God, I was in so much trouble. If these guys didn't kill me, my father would for sure. Green blurred by as I stepped on leaves, jumped over branches, and kicked up dirt. Two more bullets soared through, quick sharp zips that scared me more than I cared to admit. I ran as fast as I could, my heart and head pounding in tandem. I could feel my own pulse as I ran, my chest trying to draw in enough air to keep me going. Another gun shot rang out, but unlike the others it didn't hit a tree. A piercing and shocking white-hot pain hit my side. I went down and tumbled into a pile of leaves — crunching them under my weight — rolled back up and kept going. I covered my side with my hand, blood oozing between my fingers. I looked down and stumbled at the sight. "Oh *l'enfer.*" I breathed out the curse, pulling my hand away as it was bright red.

"Al!" Luca sing-songed, "Where's the rabbit gone now? Come out, you little *abâtardi!*"

I heard him laugh, and I knew I was losing blood. Fast. I needed a break; I need to stop. How could I? If I stopped, I could be found. If I stopped, they could shoot me. If I stopped, I could die. I spotted a gnarled tree, it's roots so big and deep it created a little cave. I skidded towards it, sliding on my back into the small hideout like I used to when I played ball with the boys in school. How long ago that seemed, how much had changed since then.

It was silent as I turned and settled for a moment in the cool underground of the tree, disrupting cobwebs and critters alike. It was big and deep enough for me to stretch out, my lungs still working to bring in the dusty air. I checked the outside again, not seeing anything I slumped down and breathed. I felt like an animal, running for my life.

If I made it out of this I would never, ever, go hunting for rabbits with my father again. Birds, squirrels, all of them wouldn't be shot by me. I chucked deliriously as I sat there bleeding, thinking about squirrels and rabbits.

I sent up a prayer before turning my attention to the bullet wound I had. "Someone shot me…" I breathed out in shock. Looking at the wound, covered in blood and dirt it didn't look good. I groaned and grit my teeth when I pulled my hand away. Blood seeped from the wound, but there wasn't a bullet lodged in there. I used my shirt, the parts that weren't already red to wipe away some of the liquid, noticing it was more of a graze than anything. I thumped my head back against the dirt in relief. *"Dieu merci."* I prayed. I rested for a moment, the forest still enough I could hear birds chirping.

Leaves rustled and I tensed, my whole body going stiff. The crunching came closer. I clenched my jaw and held my breath, trying not to make a sound.

A face popped in front of me. I started badly. It wasn't a human's face, but a fox's. It stared at me with amber colored eyes, it's beautiful coat was dark orange and black, it's ears were alert and it's poufy tail waged once. My mother's favorite animal, I recalled. The fox looked at me expectantly.

"Oh! I'm sorry, is this your home?" I asked it, chuckling a little afterwards when I realized I was talking to a fox.

It titled its head at me, studying me. I hope it didn't attack, the last thing I needed right now was to be bitten by a fox. It flicked its tail and yelped, making me flinch by the loud noise.

I put a finger to my lips, "Shh! Please, Amelia, shh!" My brain took a moment to register that I'd just named the fox after my mother, I didn't even know if it was a female fox. A vixen wasn't it? Why had I done that, instinct? Blood loss? My thoughts felt heavy and clouded.

The foxed yelped again, ears flat and flicked its tail again. I groggily realized it was only going in one direction. Left.

"What are you telling me?" I asked the animal. It yelped again and hit its left leg again with its tail. "Do you want me to go that way?" I sighed and hung my head. "You're talking to a fox, Al. An animal. It can't understand you."

The fox yelped again, mouth opening in a pant, she came closer and I froze as she burrowed under my neck. I barely breathed as her warm fur covered my throat, it was so fluffy, so soft. She nipped at my collar and pulled it.

I groaned and hit my fist against the dirt, "This is so *insensée*, it's foolish, but…" I looked at the fox in her amber colored eyes. "Alright."

I crawled out of the cave, the fox yipping excitedly. I paused as pain laced up my side, but I kept going. I started off at a jog, heading left. Amelia ran beside me for a moment before stopping and yelping at me. She wagged her tail left once and then took off, going back the way we came. I didn't question what just happened, I was letting a fox decide where I was going. She probably just wanted me out of her home, what was I doing? For some reason I kept going. I heard a voice echoing. Pausing I ducked behind a tree and looked back. The fox's den was close enough that I could still see it. Luca and Jon came up upon it, moments after I had left. The fox came barreling out of her home, a blur of black and orange as she attacked Luca's ankle. He screamed and shook his leg to get her off. I inhaled sharply, panicking, when a gunshot went off. My eyes were blown wide, and I put a hand over my mouth to keep myself from yelling when I saw the fox slump down with a pained yelp. Jon had shot her.

"*Animal fou!*" Luca spit, kicking the fox's body. Turning to Jon he ordered, "Crawl in there and see if he's in there. We cannot lose him!"

"Why do I have to do it? You're smaller." Jon protested, before Luca shoved his shoulder and he crawled into the cave.

I took that as an advantage and started running again. I cursed loudly when a stick snapped under my heel. I heard shouts from both Luca and Jon before footsteps followed me. Three pairs of feet pounded through the forest; I didn't have that much of a lead on them this time.

"There he is!" Jon shouted, coming around on my left. I skidded and turned around a tree, stopping with a slide of leaves as Luca pulled up on my right.

Luca brushed his hair back into place and smirked, straightening his suit. "Well, that was fun." He raised the revolver at me. "Now for some business."

I heard the gunshot, but I didn't die instantly like I expected. I was thrown back into a tree, sliding to the ground as my head thumped against the bark. I looked in shock at the blood seeping out of my right shoulder, I could not move my arm. I panted brokenly, trying to keep in my panic as the pain turned red then white hot and I shut my eyes tight. I screamed when a shoe pressed on the bullet still lodged in my shoulder. I peeled open my eyes and saw Luca wiping his shoe off in the grass.

"Why didn't you kill him?" Jon said, sounding far away. He nudged my foot and looked at Luca.

"*Monsieur* Koechlin said a slow death, painful." Luca grinned. "That bullet wound in his shoulder, plus his head wound, and the bullet graze...he'll bleed out soon enough."

I blinked sluggishly, my vision focusing and becoming blurry. I raised a hand tiredly to my shoulder, but I couldn't put any helpful pressure on it. I swallowed and tasted blood from the spray the bullet made piercing my flesh.

Jon and Luca were still talking, but I couldn't hear them anymore. Everything was fading, I didn't want to die. My father would be devastated, he wouldn't survive losing me. Eiffel was counting on me, he had no one else. Maurice couldn't win. I couldn't fail, not yet. I groaned faintly as I tried moving, succeeding in only slumping more against the tree. I couldn't hear anything now, the forest turning more white than green. I smiled, just a little, as I realized that maybe it would be good. I would see my mother again. I missed her. I was tired and cold. The warmth of the blood running down my side and shoulder was going away. My head rolled to the side as I let go….my hearing went completely, and my vision turned white.

Chapter Nine - Mon Garçon Préféré

"My favorite boy, it's time to wake up," That was the first thing I heard when I took in a gasping breath, shooting straight up from where I was lying on the ground.

"Mother?" I asked, my voice sounding off, high and odd for some reason. I looked around, the surrounding area I was in was a pure white, blinding white. It burned my eyes. My body didn't hurt anymore, nothing hurt at the moment. I patted down my body, feeling my side and my shoulder. My hands came away clean, bloodless.

I looked around for the voice again. "Mama!" I called, standing up, noticing that things were a lot bigger than they were last.

"Over here, my *amoureux*." My mother said, softly appearing a few feet from me. I ran to her, clutching her waist, her hands coming up to cup my hair.

I let loose a sob, "You're just as I remember you." I gushed, looking her over. Her eyes were the same as mine, her perfectly beautiful face so gentle and kind. Her hair was slightly curly, and I remembered pulling or playing with it to make her laugh or get her attention. She kissed the top of my head and warmth spread down my entire body.

"So are you!" She smiled, cupping my face between strong hands. "My little man, six years old already."

I stepped back a little, confused, I lifted my hand up to my face and saw a child's hand. I realized then that I was six again, not seventeen. I was as my mother last remembered me. I looked around us, there was nothing other than the white and my mother and I. "Where are we, Mama? Is this Heaven?"

My mother laughed, rich like pure honey, and kissed my nose. "No, my love." She walked me over to a sudden scene, the park that was near my house where my father and I still lived, a bench forming for us to sit on. She pulled me on her lap, her hug enveloping me like a babe in the womb. My hands instantly went to the fabric of her light-yellow dress, fiddling with it. "This is a visiting place, somewhere very special."

"Did I die?" I asked, the childlike voice I now had still throwing me off.

My mother's gaze looked at me softly, like she was afraid to break me by saying something. "No, you didn't. Not yet," She kissed my cheek like a butterfly's kiss. "You must go back, Aleron."

 Ruffling my hair a little she made me look at her. "My precious boy, your job isn't finished yet."

135

My face crumbled and I snuggled into her chest. "No, Mama. I want to stay here, with you."

She rocked both of us, her curly hair falling a little on my face. "I know *bébé*, I know." We were silent and just revealed in each other's embraces for a moment. She put me down in front of her, taking my small hands, and booped my nose. "My sweet boy, if you stay here what would your poor father do without you?"

I looked down at the floor. "He'd be better, he wouldn't worry or have to scold me. He'd be happier."

Mama tutted lightly, "Oh my love! That's not true!" She tucked a small piece of hair behind the shell of my ear. "Your father was never a happier man than the day you were born. He wore a hole in the floor with his pacing as you came into this world. The minute he was able to, he held you in his arms and named you."

I listened eagerly to her story. I'd never heard this before, my father had never told me stories of before I was born. "He named me?"

Mama nodded. "He did, your name, Aleron, means Eagle. He named you this because he knew you were going to reach great heights and achieve amazing things." She caught my eye. "And he was right."

I shook my head. "I failed, I messed up, Eiffel's going to die because I couldn't save him." I protested. "I don't want to go back." Tears flooded my eyes. "I miss you too much, it hurts to go back."

Mama's eyes softened with so much love I was sure it was tangible; I could touch it if I tried. "I miss you every day, your father too, and one day you'll be with me." She shook her head sadly, "But it's not today, Al. You have to fight to go back."

I shook my head, "No, don't make me." The tears left salty trails down my face.

"I want you to stay, my little bug. I do," Mama reassured me. "But," She said, gently knocking me under the chin. "If you don't go back then what was all this for? What was saving Eiffel all about? What's your purpose? And I'm fairly sure *Père* would miss your rambunctiousness."

I laughed a little, thick with tears. "I think he would too." I contemplated my mother's words. "I do have to go back...don't I?"

She kissed my forehead. "I'm sorry," Mama took off something that was around her neck. "Here, a little parting gift. I'll see you again my love, my favorite boy. My Aleron, the Eagle." She handed me a locket. I opened it and inside was a picture I'd never seen before. It held my father, dressed in his nicest suit, looking down at my mother, who was in her wedding dress. Her bouquet was in her lap as she looked up at my father, smiles on both of their faces. Mama closed the locket in my hand. "Tell your father to stop feeling guilt, show him this and tell him to *feel*." She winked. "He'll know what I mean."

I nodded. "I guess I better get back down there." I stood up and suddenly I was seventeen again. My mother was now shorter and I looked down at her a little. I laughed slightly. "What do you think?"

She had tears in her eyes, "I think I see the most amazing, *incroyable*, wonderful young man I have ever had the pleasure of knowing." She ran a hand through my hair. "Bless you, you got your father's hair, curls are terrible."

I laughed, my voice wet with tears, "Thank you, Mama." I hugged her tightly, locket digging into my hand. "I love you."

"Je t'aime aussi, bébé." She whispered back, her voice fading like the moon did as the sun started to rise. The morning dew on grass drying up with its beautiful rays, its warmth filling everything with life. My mother was this warmth and I held onto it as long as I could as I felt myself slipping back into the world full of pain and sorrow, but also joy and adventure.

Anyhow, I had something to look forward to now: seeing her again.

My mother called with one more thing. "Oh and Aleron?" She smiled. "Try not to have any other stunts like that in the woods."

I opened my mouth to reply as she got fainter. "That was you!?"

My mother winked at me, "I'll see you soon, Al. Be an eagle."

I awoke with a startling gasp, same as when I woke up to my mother, only this time I was in reality. There were hands on my chest, pushing me down. I opened my eyes and saw my uncle and father hovering over me.

"W-what happened?" I asked, settling down instead of fighting them. I looked down and saw that I was in my bed. My shoulder was wrapped, bandages around it along with my chest. My side also had bandages and my concussion was gone. "How long have I been out?" I questioned, trying to sit up. I rubbed my eyes, I was tired. *So* tired.

My father helped me, letting me lean against a few pillows that were stacked behind me. "How are you feeling, Al?" He touched my forehead where I'd gotten hit.

"I'm fine, *physically*." I answered truthfully. I moved my arm and hissed as tingles of pain raced down my shoulder. "Is my shoulder okay?"

My father and uncle looked at each other before my father answered me. "You lost a lot of blood Al, your side's going to scar, but your head is fine. You had a concussion, but it's subsided. As for your arm…" He took in a breath. "The wound got infected, the doctors had to remove a lot of infected flesh, it'll be a nasty looking scar and you'll need to exercise it, but you've lost some of your mobility." He explained, face pinched as he told me the results of my injuries.

I furrowed my brows. "How much mobility?" I questioned, voice low.

"Try moving your right hand." My uncle suggested, pulling it free from the blankets.

I did as he asked, moving my fingers slightly but when I tried making a fist my fingers only curled a little, looking like a claw. "What?" I turned towards my father, tearing my eyes away from my hand. It was the hand I wrote with, the hand I hunted with, my dominant hand. Could I still use it? Was it crippled? My breathe didn't want to be drawn into my lungs and the hand that wasn't working started trembling.

My father shushed me, "Calm down, son, calm down. It's okay. You can still move your arm, the bullet shattered the bone. The doctors did what they could."

"What happened?" I demanded, taking off the stupid head bandages I just realized I had on. My other side was fine, it was tender but it *had* just been a graze. I winced as I stretched to see my shoulder. The bandages were the dull sickly green color of scabbing and infection.

My father sighed and began to explain, "Clarisse found you. By the time we got help.....you nearly died. The doctor couldn't find your heartbeat. You *did* die Aleron." He pinched his nose, and I knew he was holding back tears. It was the first sign he did. "Then you gasped awake, like the life had been thrown back into you."

He ruffled my hair, eyes bright with unshed tears. "You fought to come back, you lost so much blood. It was coating the grass, your clothes, the tree. *Mon Dieu,* it'll scar me forever — that image of you."

He kissed my head. "When we got you home, the doctors started working on you, your arm and your side. You got a raging fever after they took the bullet out, we thought you were going to die again. Somehow you managed not to, you've been unconscious until now." He explained.

"How did Clarisse find me?" I asked, taking in the information my father gave me.

My father shook his head, "She wouldn't say. She left before we could question her, then my focus was on you."

I blinked in dismay then I nodded, I suspected there wouldn't be an answer from Clarisse. At least not yet. "How long ago was that?"

My father's eyes slipped from mine, he clenched his jaw. "Two weeks ago."

"What?!" I screeched, my voice breaking at its high pitch. I'd been out for two weeks, I paled suddenly my heart dropping. "Please... tell me Eiffel is alive."

My uncle nodded and I let out a breath of relief. "No one has heard from him in a few days, last he was seen he was alive." Uncle François told me, looking doubtful.

"I know who did this!" I protested, throwing the blankets back. Trying to get out of bed but failed, my side stretching painfully.

"Then let's take it to the authorities. Aleron, you almost died. You did die! Let someone else handle it!" My father scolded me, shoving me back into the bed.

I shook my head, "No! He has people in the police force under his thumb."

"Aleron! Sit down!" My father yelled at me, quite forcefully.

I understood my father's concern, but I had to get through to him. "You're right, I *did* die." I hesitated then, "I saw her." I told him, stopping him in his tracks.

My father turned to my uncle. "Can we have a moment of privacy please?"

Uncle François left, looking at us suspiciously. "Of course."

My father sat down on the side of my bed, looking at me. "What do you mean you saw her?"

"I saw her *père*." I started, "I saw my mother, she was *beautiful*. She was...exactly as I remembered her to be. She saved me in the woods, and she told me to go back when I wanted to stay with her." I could tell I caught my father off guard, taking a moment to remember I told him about the visit I had with my mother, about the fox in the woods, and about fighting to wake up here. "She saved me, Father." I scrambled suddenly to prove it, "Wait, wait, she gave me something to

141

show you." I rummaged through the bed covers and blankets, I found what I was looking for. "Here." I said softly, giving my father the locket.

My father touched the locket reverently, running a finger over its oval edge. He clenched it in his fist and held it to his chest. It was the only time I'd ever seen my father cry. Not just cry but sob. I didn't know what to do, I didn't expect this. I put a hand, somewhat awkwardly, on my father's shoulder. "She told me to tell you to feel."

My father only cried harder after I told him that, it was like his grief was fresh and raw, old wounds reopened unexpectedly. He crushed me in a hug, a rare show of fatherly affection.

He calmed down a little when I hugged him back, his shoulders not shaking so much as the tears subsided. He opened the locket and smiled at the picture. "Ami, my love." He showed me the image again. "I gave this to her before she got sick. She never took it off." He sniffed. "It's a miracle, Aleron." He chuckled wetly, "Of course, she told me to feel."

I laughed a little. "What does that even mean?"

My father closed the locket, handing it back to never so carefully. "Your mother would always tell me to feel. To be in the moment, to feel the softness of a flower's pedal, to feel the rain on my face, to feel the warmth of the sun." My father's smile grew as he explained. "Your mother would always tell me to feel her love for me, to feel my sorrow when she got sick, to feel the joy I had in you, my boy, when you were an infant and a child." He nodded. "It's about time I started to feel again."

I smiled, before suddenly sobering. "Father, what day is it?" He told me and I groaned into my hands. "*Merde*, I was afraid of that."

"What's wrong, Al?" My father asked, titling his head.

"I have a day to save Gustave Eiffel. *One* day. Time has officially run out." I was doomed. *Ce que j'allais faire maintenant?*

Chapter Ten - Un Jour

One day— that's all that was left. Upon my father's insistence we headed to the police force, even though I told him repeatedly that Maurice had contacts within the force.

They put my arm in a sling for now, I glared at the limb every chance I had. Like I'd expected, the minute the officers saw myself, my father, and uncle we were *escorted* out. Claims of disturbing the peace on our tails.

I held my shoulder as I stood in front of the police building, "Forget it, I'm going myself."

My father tsked his tongue, "Aleron, wait just a moment." He looked at his brother. "François, maybe we could persuade them without Aleron there."

My uncle nodded, "It's worth a try, Jacques."

My father put a hand against my shoulder, "Stay here, we'll try one more time." With that they went back inside and I was left standing there.

I wanted to yell at them. To scream that we didn't have time to fool around anymore. There was no cushion to soften the blow. Time was up. I had hours, if that, to find Maurice. I didn't have time to wait and see if people would help. I rubbed my eyes with my free hand and started walking. I didn't have a destination...yet.

"Aleron!"

I spun at my name. Clarisse stood timidly behind me.

"What do you want, Clarisse?" I asked, not looking at her in the eye. "How did you get out of there?" I asked, suddenly remembering.

Clarisse bit her lip, eyes downcast, "When you got taken...it ended up loosening the bonds. The house was empty when I got out of the basement. It was terrifying."

"I'm sure," I replied, my gaze far off in the distance as I listened to her words.

"When I heard the gunshot....I was scared to *death*. I actually screamed. I knew it had to do with you." She looked at me and stepped forward to clasp my hand. "I didn't know what they were going to do to you. I nearly left, but...I swear-"

"You didn't have to save me, Clarisse!" I shouted at her, wanting her to know how much I was hurt by her choices and her betrayal. "So, why did you then?"

She let go of my hand like it burned her. "You're right, Aleron. I didn't have to save you!" Clarisse's gaze finally met mine. "But I couldn't let you die either."

I pulled my hand away from her, turning to walk away. "If you had not betrayed me I wouldn't have nearly died."

"I did what I had to do!" Her face grew angry. "You know why I made those choices, why I helped Maurice...my father-"

I cut her off again. "Yes! Yes, I know, Clarisse. You made your reason abundantly clear." I shook my head and walked away. I was stopped by my sleeve getting tugged on.

"You're leaving me?" Clarisse asked, softly, anger gone from her face and now I could read every unfiltered emotion on her face. The thoughts almost tangible in her eyes.

I glared at her as an answer, my heart clenching in my chest and making my stomach queasy. I clenched my jaw, and my shoulder ached like someone rubbed dirt into the wound just to accentuate the hurt I felt.

Clarisse let go of my sleeve and wrung her hands, looking down at our feet. She laughed mirthlessly, the sound unlike anything I'd ever heard from her before. "You did say that you could never trust anyone to stay."

It hurt to have my own words thrown back at me, the words I told in a private emotional moment replayed in my head. I sniffed and cleared my throat, tucking my hand in my pocket and looked away from her face. "Well, I thought you would be the exception."

Clarisse let out a small hurt noise at this. It was hard to ignore.

"Goodbye, Clarisse." I told her, hesitating for a moment before coming close and kissing her cheek. It was quick but with it, I put as much regret and emotion as I could muster.

She gripped my shirt. "Al... I'm sorry…" Her blue eyes met mine, and I wondered if I could ever look at them the same way again. "I love you." She said. So softly it was like a whispered breath, the kind that blew away dandelions filled with wishes.

I looked at our closeness, nearly chest to chest, my throat closed as I couldn't say the words back. No matter how badly I wanted to. *Maudire l'amour.* I shook my head, "I don't believe you." I whispered, just as broken and just as soft. It took every ounce of my will to pull away from her, to turn around...and to not look back.

✶✶✶

I made my way to Eiffel's hotel, half my mind stuck on Clarisse and the other half trying to figure out what Maurice's next move was. There was less than a day before the deadline, Eiffel must be nervous. It was hopefully the reason why no one had seen him in a few days. I hoped that he'd become a temporary hermit until this matter was resolved. I went to knock on the hotel door, having made my way slowly up all the stairs and having to pause multiple times because of the stitches in my side. My hand grazed the door, just slightly and it opened...it looked like it was never full closed.

"*Oh non c'est pas bon,*" I mumbled, dread flooding me. I pushed open the door. My gaze went instantly to Eiffel's usual chair, but it was empty. Was he here? Did he move rooms? Change hotels? I walked further into the room, hackles raised and wished I had better hearing. There was a scuffle near the sitting room, I walked that way, taking hesitant steps and finally spotted Eiffel. His eyes were wide and terrified, his body was roped to a chair, the bonds cutting into his arms and legs through his suit. He had a gag in his mouth that was cutting off muffled yells. His hair was disheveled, and his nose looked broken. Blood was running down his face from a cut against his temple.

He was shaking his head at me and trying to speak through the gag. For a moment I stood frozen then I urged myself forward. Coming closer and took it out of his mouth, loosening it so the gag hung around his neck.

"*Monsieur* Eiffel, are you okay?" I asked, trying to work against the bonds with just one hand.

Gustave shook his head and opened his mouth to reply, eyes going wide.

I turned around right as fire ignited between my injured shoulder and my neck. I went down to the ground with a pained shout. I looked up, glaring at Maurice who held the butt of a gun in his hand.

"Oh, you're still alive." He said, looking down at me with a raised eyebrow.

I put a hand against my shoulder, still on the floor. "Don't sound so disappointed, I might start thinking you don't like me." I half snarked half groaned at him.

Maurice laughed. "You're right Aleron, I don't like you." He circled me like a hunting dog about to take down its prey. "You couldn't have waited a few moments," He raised the gun and pointed it towards me. "I was about to pull the trigger, Al."

I just glared at him, silently daring him to do so. He'd failed once already. I'd like to see him push his luck.

Maurice tsked, cocking the revolver. The click ominous.

"Maurice, stop it! *Mon Dieu*, he's just a boy! I'm the one you want to kill, leave Aleron out of it." Gustave Eiffel protested, protesting to get Maurice's attention.

"Why are you doing this?" I asked, pulling myself up a little so I wasn't vertical on the floor. I scooted backwards until I hit the wall, leaning against it. "What is all this for?"

It was like I set off an explosion. Maurice went red with rage and he started waving the gun around, still loaded. Gustave was still stuck in his chair and I was being held in the middle of the room at gunpoint.

"This! This all happened because of him!" Maurice started, shoving the gun in Eiffel's face. "We worked together on this Eiffel tower of his, in fact *I* was the one that drew up the original blueprint. The *original* draws and plans, then this *abâtardi*had to steel it from me!" He pointed to himself with both hands. "Does anyone know who *I* am, no! He took all the credit, the fame, the glory, the recognition, and left me in the dust to follow like a dog."

I watched Maurice get more and more agitated, the calm composer that I had seen the man all those times before now gone and in its place was someone who'd thought about revenge longer than was healthy. Years of pent up emotions and feelings giving ammunition to Maurice's words. Eiffel was Maurice's obsession, greed the flame to the fire.

Maurice took a step back from Gustave, looking at him with dead eyes and a heated gaze. "I'm the one who won that contest for you Gustave, yet you betrayed me and stole my idea."

Gustave didn't say anything, looking at his friend with wide petrified eyes. "If I'd known it would have won, I would have mentioned your name-"

"It's too late for that now!" Maurice yelled, "I worked on that tower, the *Tour de three hundred mètres*."

I scooted closer to Eiffel, inching along the wall to keep out of the way. My shoulder ached painfully, sharp pains of ice and fire racing down my arm. It was warm with blood, wounds reopened. I watched Maurice stare at Eiffel, almost like a deadly staring contest. A gunshot rang out and I startled badly, ducking, the sound making my ears ring. I looked down and the floor was smoldering where I'd just been. The hole in the floor was near my hand and I looked up into the still smoking barrel of the gun. I couldn't help the gulp that I did.

"Don't move Aleron, you're distracting." Maurice told me with a scowl. "I only have five left now."

Turning his attention back to Eiffel, Maurice explained to me why he was doing the assassination plot, the cause of it.

"Now, Gustave here, he retired from his company. From his projects. Handed me the Tower and didn't think anything of it." He looked at me and grinned. "Little did this man know that it was going to win." Maurice popped the barrel out of the revolver and spun it, "Once it won, Gustave took it back. Claiming it was his idea at the start, never mind he was retired and out of the company. Never mind he'd placed me in charge, and never mind that he didn't come up with the idea." He pointed the gun at Eiffel, which made the man shy away from it. "There went the glory, the recognition, and in came Gustave Eiffel so proud of his winning project." Maurice pulled the trigger.

I gasped when it clicked — the one empty bullet chamber that it had just saved Eiffel's life. My heart jackhammered in my chest, my wide eyes meeting Eiffel's as we both just registered that fate had let Eiffel have a few more minutes to live.

"Greed? That's why you're going this Maurice?" Eiffel asked, I could see his own panicked breaths from where I was against the wall next to him. "You want to kill me over recognition? This is *aliéné*! Crazy!" He protested, tryingto show reason to his friend. "Let Aleron go, let *me* go, and this will all go away. I'll add your name, I'll make sure you're mentioned."

I wanted to slap my forehead at Gustave's stupidity. From Maurice's face I could tell that that was not what he wanted, that wasn't enough. I wanted to tell Gustave to just give him the whole project, you greedy man! I rolled my eyes at Eiffel's words, both were greedy pig-headed men that wanted nothing more than their names to do down in history attached to something great. What they didn't realize is that a lot of men and women went down in history without ever having their names known. My mother was one of them, my father too. I'd gotten trapped in between the incredibly childish feud between having fame and being forgotten.

Maurice moved and put the gag back in Gustave's mouth, much to the other's displeasure and muffled protests started. "That's not the right answer, Gustave." Maurice insisted, pointing the revolver at Eiffel again. "I need you gone so I can fully take over the company *and* the Tower."

I took my chance then, rushing Maurice in the side, taking him down with me to the floor. The gun discharged when it hit the ground, shooting the bullet into the corner of the ceiling. Crumbled plaster from the ceiling rained down on us, covering us in lookalike snow. I scrambled with Maurice, but he had two fully working arms and shoved me to the side. He crawled to the gun, but as adrenaline started rushing through my system, the fighting that I was so used to in school and in life started kicking in. I pulled off my sling and wrapped it around Maurice's neck, pulling it tight. I pulled him backwards and wrapped my legs around his torso, putting him in a lock as I choked him. The man was larger than me and it was costing me a lot of strength to keep him there, strength I didn't quite have. Maurice got an elbow to my still healing side and I released him coughing for breath. Ugly crimson started running down my side.

Maurice grabbed my shirt and pulled me backwards, away from the gun. I kicked him and fought, yelling and shouting. He dug his thumb into my shoulder and I screamed as white hot agony raged through my veins, my arm going numb for a moment. Maurice stood up on shaky legs, hand still rubbing at his throat and started reaching for the gun.

"No!" I dug into myself, reaching for the will to move. Remembering my mother's words, I found it and gripped it like a lifeline. I coughed harshly as I rolled over and blindly reached for something. I found a thick volume that had fallen off a shelf in Maurice and Gustave's initial struggle. I picked it up and threw it, hitting Maurice in the side of the head, knocking him off course and the book landed with a thud next to him. Thanking every saint possible I pushed myself to my feet, skidding on my knees to get the gun. I wrapped my hand around it and spun around at Maurice's enraged yell. We were inches apart. I could see his dark empty eyes and the snarl on his face. A boom went off.

Maurice paused with a shocked look on his face and looked down at the blooming flower of red on his chest. He dropped the black iron fireplace poker that was in his hand, which he intended to stab me with, a clatter ringing out as it hit the floor. Maurice's body fell forward and it landed on top of me.

I panicked as I struggled underneath his weight with just one hand to push him off. His warm blood trickled onto my clothes. I whimpered a little as I worked to get the body off of me. *Mon Dieu*, I hadn't meant to pull the trigger, I didn't mean to… Oh God. I didn't even know I'd pulled the trigger. I killed him, I-I killed Maurice Koechlin. *La Bête* was dead. *Mon Dieu*, help me. It had just been a reaction.

I shoved Maurice's body off with a cut off cry. Bile curled in my throat and I couldn't breath. The gun was still in my hand...I scrambled to my feet with tears in my eyes, walking towards Eiffel to release him from the ropes.

Taking off Eiffel's gag I said, "I'm sorry…" I looked over at Maurice's still body. I started working on the bonds behind the chair that entrapped Eiffel's hands. It took some time, but I managed to undo them. Eiffel was free — he was safe. Together we made quick work of the rest of the ropes.

"Aleron, look at me." Gustave said, rubbing his wrists once he was fully free of the chair.

I looked at him, still seeing the body in the corner of my eye.

"It was self-defense Aleron, that's all it was. I'll make sure of it." Gustave reassured me, at least he tried to. He put a gentle hand on my non-injured shoulder. "I owe you my life, my lad. *Merci*. Thank you." His eyes met mine and I saw the gratitude he had, the thanks, and the joy. I also saw the sadness he had for losing his friend and I saw the depths of someone who knew hurt, sometimes it was fresher than others. I was viewing his soul in that moment.

I saw myself.

I nodded my head. *"Vous êtes les bienvenus."*

Eiffel gave my shoulder a squeeze. "You'll be rewarded Aleron, I promise."

"That's not why I did it." I protested. "You don't need to reward me."

Eiffel shook his head, "Nonsense Al, I think you'll like it."

Before I could protest some more thundering steps were heard coming up towards the room. I tensed, before the door opened and in came my father. My uncle was less than a step behind him. They came in with four or five officers behind them. It looks like they found some good guys on the force.

"Aleron!" My father yelled, worried and startled, no doubt noticing my appearance. The blood surrounding my shirt, the pulled stitches on my side, the arm loose from its sling. The dead body in the corner and the terrible mess of several scuffles.

He came over to me and cupped the back of my head as he tucked me against his chest. I didn't know how much I needed that comfort until I had it. I sunk into his touch.

"It's not mine." I explained, talking about the blood.

The officers started taking charge of the situation, their voices drowning out the feelings that were mixing in my chest. I clung onto my father, hearing and focusing on his heart beating steadily underneath my ear. For the first time in months I relaxed, I'd done it. Gustave Eiffel was saved. Hewouldn't die and the Eiffel Tower would get built. I'd managed to save him, *je l'ai fait.*

Oh God, I was so tired, my body felt weak and numb. My muscles and mind finally relaxed now that I firmly knew I could allow them to. My knees went weak and I crumbled to the ground, my father's startled yell of my name following me into oblivion.

Chapter Eleven - Les Journaux

*The newspapers*ran the story all through the next week.Everywhere I looked I read headlines about what had happened. Eiffel's face on the front page every time. After interviewing both Eiffel and I, the police took over my investigation taking the credit for it. Once I had awoken from when I'd passed out, the cause was mostly shock and malnutrition of my own doing. The police finally decided to take me seriously.

Eiffel and I told them the entire story, with both my father, Alex, my uncle, and even Clarisse used as accountable witnesses to the entire plot. Plus the body of Maurice Koechlin still in the room, we were allowed to go home.

The newspapers were quick to roll out the story from their printing presses and as I'd wished I remained the anonymous rescuer of the entire thing. I hadn't done it for the glory, for the fame, or even the recognition of saving Gustave Eiffel. I did it because a man's life was in danger. After what Maurice had told me I wasn't sure if I could call Eiffel innocent anymore. Maurice's story was blatantly told by the winners of the tale, by Eiffel. Maurice was blasphemed, his name dragged through the mud, and his reputation was in shambles. People who didn't even know the man or the Koechlin family suddenly had opinions and thoughts upon the man. How hypocritical society truly is?

I felt guilty and I didn't know why.

I was walking around town, noticing nearly everyone's noses were stuck into a newspaper, still hot off the press, eating up the story that was no doubt elaborated to gain more readers. It was two days after the incident had happened. After the deadline had passed and after I had shot someone in self-defense. I felt as if that would stay with me long after the story faded from people's minds. My father still tried to comfort me after I'd told him how *I'd* been the one to shoot Maurice. Logically, I knew that if I hadn't protected myself, more than likely I would've been dead. For good this time. I shuddered every time I thought of Maurice's gaze, his dead eyes haunting my nights, as he fell to the ground on top of me.

155

My shoulder still ached and hurt from my escapade and the struggles I had. My side had to get re-stitched and I'd had enough concussions to last my entire life. My arm was still in a sling, but I could still feel the imaginary blood that was running down it especially at night. My father said sometimes h heard me talking in my sleep after dreams in the middle of the night. I still felt exhausted, hyper-alert even thought I *knew* that the danger had passed.

"Wait up, Al!" I heard someone yell. Other times when people had yelled my name replayed in my mind and make me tense. I turned my head, my new newsboy hat blocking the midday sun from my eyes. I did a double take when I saw Val and Tomas coming up beside me.

Val waved the copy of the newspaper he had in his hands, his face remorseful. He cleared his throat and the three of us stared at each other in awkward silence.

Tomas and Val looked at each other before Tomas stepped forward and offered me his hand. "We're sorry we did not believe you Al. If you could...could you forgive us?"

I looked at my friend's hand. Former friend? I clenched my jaw a few times thinking. Not once did they ever leave me in the past. Until this Eiffel assassination plot had showed up. I now knew that they weren't as friendly or as loyal as I had thought. I'd needed them to be by my side and that's when they decided to leave it. It hurt to think that we once had a bond, a close bond. At times I wished for both of them to be my brothers. Now...they were distant, faces of a time well past. I wanted to say no. No, that I did not forgive them. I didn't want to. My heart was still bruised and beaten from Clarisse, but I knew that I needed to forgive them if I was going to move on. And I did. I did want to move on, I wanted to forget most of what happened, even when I couldn't. I didn't regret saving Gustave Eiffel, I regretted the many things that it took to get there.

156

I took Tomas's hand, squeezing it, remembering the last time we were face to face. "I forgive you, both of you," I said, actually feeling the truth in the words, which surprised me. *"Au revoir."* I nodded at them, turning and left. I had someplace to be.

I headed towards the coaches. The stagecoach depot that took people in and out of Paris and in and out of France in general. I hung back for a moment, watching the Alix family, Clarisse's family, putting trunks onto the top of the coach. Clarisse and her mother stood off to the side, small parasols and bonnets in perfect order. She was leaving. Leaving Paris, leaving Maurice behind her, leaving her father's debt, and leaving me. My head and heart were at war with each other, every *single* time I thought of her. It was hard not to; I'd once loved her. I had just never had the opportunity to show her that. The men were just finishing putting all of the luggage on the coach when Clarisse's mother got in and she followed behind. Her father talked with the coachman and I saw that this was my chance.

"Clarisse!" I called, voice low but it still carried. I walked over to the window of the coach where she was. I couldn't leave without saying goodbye to her. The snorting horses in the front of the coach were loud enough to cover our conversation.

Clarisse's eyes widened just a little at seeing me, she leaned a little out of the coach, so her mother didn't see me. "Aleron….what are you doing here?"

I avoided her question, asking one of my own. "Where are you going?"

Clarisse bit her lip, eyes downcast. "We're heading to stay with my brother Paul. I-I don't know...if we'll come back."

I felt like I was kicked in the chest when I heard her actually say those words. I didn't want to believe them, but now they were out there for fate to decide. I swallowed thickly, cleaning my throat. "I hope...I hope you find a better life there." I finally decided to say.

Clarisse met my gaze. Both of us saying things that we knew we couldn't out loud just by our eyes. There was an air of anagapesis around us. It was like the whole moment died down for the two of us, the birds were silent, no noises to bother us. Those that could be heard were muffled, unspoken words were clear, and silence roared. Clarisse looked away first.

The coachman yelled that he was taking off and I knew our time had ended.

Clarisse's eyes filled with tears and she kissed her fingertips, "*Pardonne-moi.*" She whispered, delicately placing her palm against my cheek.

How different I felt when Clarisse asked for my forgiveness, versus Val and Tomas. I turned into the hand against my cheek, seeing the coachman climb up to the reins and flick his whip. I took a step away from the coach, pulling away from Clarisse and put my hand in my pocket. I watched the coach pick up speed and leave. I knew in my heart — could feel it in my bones — that I would never see her again. Still...I couldn't forgive her. I stood there watching her leave until her coach was just a small brown dot on the horizon.

"*Qui n'avance pas, recule.*" I told her ghost, Alex's words that he once told me. Those who do not move forward, recede. We were moving forward, only in different directions. I raised myself straight and tall, lifting my hand up in a flourish and bowed at the waist, giving her a proper French gentleman's goodbye. I wished her all the luck in the world and that fate and God be kind to her. "*Jusqu'à ce que nous nous revoyions, ce destin est bon."* I said in farewell. Until we meet again...this fate was good. I never saw Clarisse again.

✳✳✳

Months and weeks passed until it was May 5th, 1889. The World's Fair made it to Paris. The *Exposition Universelle de 1889.* I stood on the tallest level of the Eiffel Tower, having been completed two months prior. It was now shining over Paris. Gustave Eiffel had invited me to his private apartment at the top, he said he had an interesting proposition for me. From there I could see the whole of Paris, my beautiful city. The Exposition was taking up most of the buildings and people were tiny ants walking underneath me. Eiffel had told me that the World's Fair was held in Paris to celebrate the anniversary of the Storming of Bastille. The grounds were filled with hundreds, thousands, of people coming from all over to visit and see Eiffel's greatest project. I couldn't believe that he was going to demolish it after the fair was over. A contract with the city allowed it to stand until 1909, barely twenty years. As Eiffel had told me that it was for the fair only. It was never going to be permanent.

"A beautiful sight, no?" Eiffel said, coming to stand next to me where I was staring out of the apartment window, looking down at the exhibits of the fair.

I nodded. The sloping roofs of the buildings of the exhibits shined in the setting sun, the already illuminated gardens and restaurants gave a lingering romantic feel to them. The Fair was staying until October of that year then taking off for the next country. I had plans to go with Alex to visit the *Galerie des Machines*, an architect's playground, near the end of the Exposition grounds later that day.

"*Monsieur*," I asked, putting a pause to my thoughts for now. "Why did you want me here?" I turned away from the window and faced him.

Eiffel chuckled at my bluntness, his salt and pepper hair now a little more grey than black. He'd healed fully from the accident with Maurice Koechlin and the assassination attempt. He was back to being the arrogant man everyone thought he was — brushing the entire thing behind him like dust off his shoulder. Maybe he did it with such ease because he had won, had gotten his way. Maybe it was because he hadn't shot a man.

Meanwhile. my own shoulder never fully healed. The scar that became of it was ugly and brought back painful memories. With my hand I was able to regain most of my strength, but it was much weaker than my other hand, it shook often. I stuffed it in my pocket as it started shaking now.

"I want to offer you a job," Eiffel suggested, "A true architect's job."

I was surprised, excited, but also weary. Eventually, I shook my head. "Please, you've done enough already. You've rewarded me plenty."

My reward had been my name etched into the metal of the Eiffel Tower, along with seventy-one other architects, mathematicians, scientists, and engineers that contributed to the Eiffel Tower project. The name Arago was permanently labeled on the South-East side of the tower. If anyone thought about it they would see that it was for my uncle, François Arago, who worked along with Gustave Eiffel on his tower. No one would think twice about Aleron Arago. Eiffel had planned it that way. It had simply been my duty to save him, I didn't need a reward. My own curiosity had been sated. It was never for recognition, but Eiffel said he had to pay me back somehow. By adding my name to the side of the project I'd helped save he seemed to think it fit.

"I could get your name out there Aleron, give you a start in the architect and engineering world." Eiffel offered, raising an eyebrow. "You could work with me on the next project I'm planning."

I gave him a thankful smile but shook my head. "*Merci*, but I'll have to decline. I'm fine being a boy from Paris, I'm fine with my apprentice job at Alex's shop." I stood and smiled out at the window. "I'm fine being just Aleron Arago, *Monsieur*." I shook my head a little. "I don't think that needs to change."

Eiffel studied me for a moment. "I've never met anyone quite like you, Aleron." He held out his hand. "It was a pleasure to know you."

I shook his hand, a small blush from his praise making me embarrassed. "Thank you." I headed towards the door of his apartment.

"Oh and Aleron?" Eiffel called.

I turned, my hand on the doorknob. "Yes?"

Gustave Eiffel smiled at me. "Keep asking questions."

I gave a laugh, "That's what got me in trouble in the first place." I nodded my goodbye and exited his apartment. I made my way towards a lift, passing dozens of people that had climbed the tower to see the view. I traveled down the three floors until I reached the bottom. Walking out into the crisp air, I inhaled deeply, relaxing. I looked up at the magnificent beast of metal, seeing my name emblazoned on the side, shining proudly as the sun hit it just right. I looked around the dozens of milling people around me. After the assassination, merely days after, it was old news. The rumors turned out to be true and everyone forgot about it within two weeks. No one knew what I had done, other than my father, my uncle, Clarisse, Eiffel, and myself. Maurice Koechlin lived on in his children, his wife hadn't been heard from since she took her family and moved back to Switzerland. They were the only other witnesses who knew of what occurred. The police and authorities still couldn't find them.

My father and I were back to being the only people living in our house. My uncle François had left by train back to his own hometown, shortly after the Tower's completion. Except for the ruined shoulder of mine, the memories of those who knew about it, and the grave that held Koechlin's name, it was as if none of it had even happened....it was back to the way things had started.

The only change was that I was vastly different than when I first began my journey of saving Gustave Eiffel. Now I knew the dangers the world had to offer, the dangers of greed and deceit. I was smarter, stronger, a little wearier, but overall...I was older. I was now eighteen and, yes, that might still seem young. However, my mind and heart were older than my body could ever be. I had loved and lost. I didn't fight anymore because I knew what fighting for myself felt like. I focused on my apprenticeship because it brought me joy. I was closer to my father because I nearly lost him. I saw life as precious because I had died and lived to tell the tale. I learned loyalty — the hard way — and I learned that never ever should you eavesdrop. *Ever.*

I got home that night, exhausted, but happy, and more than anything filled with a sense of relief and accomplishment. Before going to bed, I pulled out my journal. I'd been writing this story down. It was coming to a close, the journal nearly filled. I had barely a few pages left.

My name was Aleron Arago. In the summer of 1888 in Paris France, I saved a man. His name was Gustave Eiffel. I had accomplished what I had set out to do, the only thing now was to continue living. Sometimes that's the hardest part... To have some final words, I think I should say this:

Life, fate, and God all have a plan for everyone, for me. Mine was to save Gustave Eiffel, to be my father's son, and to be my mother's. To have loved and lost Clarisse Alix. Everyone has a plan and sometimes life upheaves it. Turns it upside down and backwards and still you somehow manage to come out on top. It takes courage to live. To go on an adventure. For me my question is this, "What comes next?" The only way for me to find out is if I spread my wings...

and be an eagle.

Vivre fièrement la vie,

Aleron Arago

Chapter Twelve - Ses Vieux Os

Paris, France 1951

His old bones creaked like the attic's stairs as he made his way up there. Aleron could hear the sounds of children's' laughter. The angelic fairy bells of a little one giggling. He stuck his head into the attic, "What are you three doing up here?"

Several shocked and surprised squeals came out of the three kids. Having gotten caught at being up in the attic after their parents had told them not to.

Martin, the oldest at thirteen, had a huge grin on his youthful face. *"Grandpère!"* He tugged the trunk of items closer to Aleron who'd fully climbed into the attic and had sat down on the floor. "Look what we found!"

Aleron chuckled at his grandson, "I see you found my trunk from when I was a boy."

Ami, the second oldest at nine, brought him a closed, worn, leather journal. "We found this, *Grandpère,* but it's all in French so we can't read it."

Aleron tapped his granddaughter's nose. "You would've known more French if your mother hadn't married your American father." He joked as he had numerous times before. Aleron flipped through the journal, remembering all that he'd written down as if it had happened yesterday and not sixty-two years ago. "This is my journal from when I was only eighteen years old." He explained to Ami, named after her great-grandmother and so much like her Aleron's heart ached.

"Eighteen!? But that was sooooo long ago." Martin complained, pulling his younger sister Clarisse into his lap.

Aleron laughed, running a hand through his now grey hair. "Yes, it was." He ruffled Martin's auburn hair, something the boy had gotten from his father. "Would you like me to read it to you?"

Martin and Ami's faces both lit up, excitement in their eyes. Clarisse was only six, but she nodded along with her siblings. "Yes, please!" Both of their voices answered.

Aleron nodded, he couldn't help but tease them a little. "Are you sure you want to hear such an *old* story?"

Ami rolled her eyes, ""*Grandpère! Please!*"

Giving a small laugh he obliged his grandchildren. "And in French?"

Ami bit her lip, a habit she got from her Aleron's daughter, who in turn had gotten it from Aleron. Martin raised his hand wildly as he knew the answer, but Aleron made him wait.

"*Oui-* umm *Oui- sss'il v-vous plaît?*" Ami answered hesitantly, her grandfather mouthing the words along with her as she went.

"*Excellent, mon cher!*" Aleron complemented. He opened the book, the spine cracking. "Now where shall we begin?" He paused as he remembered his past life.

"At Once Upon a Time, Grandpa," Clarisse said, coming over and sitting in Aleron's lap.

Aleron cuddled his granddaughter close, kissing her blonde head. "Of course, silly grandpa." Martin settled into Aleron's right side, careful of Aleron's shoulder. It still acted up when it rained. Ami settled on his left, laying her small head on his arm.

"Wait, wait, is this a *true* story?" Martin asked, pulling away.

Aleron nodded. "Everything in here is completely true. I wrote it down to remember it because it happened to me so long ago."

He squinted at the old writing as he remembered parts that weren't exactly child friendly.

Martin smiled, his grandson looking so much like Aleron's younger self. "This is going to be a good story then."

Aleron laughed, "The best." He opened the journal and cleared his throat, automatically translating the French he loved to the English his grandchildren knew. "I should not have listened. Let us just say that before I continue telling you my story. As I now know, you should never eavesdrop. Never. Yet I did, and this journey was created because of that. My story is one that started accidentally. It involves good times and bad times, romance and betrayal, truth and lies. I've decided to write it down because...well someone should know it. Someone should know the truth behind some things, I mean everyone wants to have their story written right? So let me take you back to the summer when I was seventeen years old..."

Glossary:

Words and phrases in order of appearance.

French to English translation.

Cochon dégoûtant	Disgusting pig
Ma charmante dame	My lovely lady
Merci	Thank you
Magnifique	Magnificent
Dieu Merci	Thank God
Monsieur	Mister
Père	Father
Oui	Yes
Imbéciles	Fools
Mon Dieu	My God
Le Comité de Trois Cents	The Committee of Three Hundred

Mère	Mother
Vous fauteur de troubles	You trouble maker
Ta gueule	Shut up
Excusez-moi	Excuse me
Quelle pagaille	What a mess
Bonjour	Hello
Allons-y	Let's go
Les jeunes	Young people
Potins	Gossips
Mon garçon préféré	My favorite boy

Le poste de police	Police station
J'ai mal a la tête	I have a headache
Bonne chance à toi	Good luck to you
Que Dieu soit avec vous	May God be with you
Au revoir mon ami	Goodbye my friend
Je t'en prie, non	Please, no
Maudit	Damn
Je suis tellement désolé, pardonne-moi	I'm so sorry, forgive me
Merde	Crap
Ma belle	My beautiful

Incroyable	Unbelievable
C'est incroyable pour moi	This is unbelievable to me
Môme	Kid
Visage rougissant	Blushed faced
Ma parole	My word
Garçon	Boy
Pardonne moi	Forgive me
La bête	The beast
Que faites-vous	What are you doing
Je suis désolé	I am sorry

Ç'est ce que ç'est	It is what it is
Zut	Damn, heck
C'est la vie ma chérie	That is life, my darling
Belle	Beautiful
Merde sainte	Holy crap
Oh L'enfer	Oh Hell
Insensée	Foolish, insane
Animal fou	Crazy animal
Amoureux	Love
Bébé	Baby

Je t'aime aussi	I love you too
Ce que j'allais faire maintenant	What was I going to do now
Maudire l'amour	Curse love
Oh non c'est pas bon	Oh no that's not good
Abâtardi	Bastard
Aliéné	Insane
Vous êtes les bienvenus	You are welcome
Je l'ai fait	I did it
Qui n'avance pas, recule	Those who do not go forward, recede.
Jusqu'à ce que nous nous revoyions, ce destin est bon	Until we meet again, this fate is good

Author's Note

"I ought to be jealous of the Tower. She is more famous than I am."

~Gustave Eiffel

Hello dear reader, first off thank you for reading this book! I hope that you enjoyed it and will share it with your friends.

Let me say, again, that anything that is not historically correct is from the author's imagination. Some of the real-life characters were younger, older, or even deceased in reality. I took artist liberties and changed ages to fit the timeline of the novel, as well as place some of them in the same city.

Maurice Koechlin is in no way a villain as I made him out to be, his architectural accomplishments are astonishing and his work with Gustave Eiffel is still standing today. His wife and children's names are historically accurate. Maurice Koechlin died in 1946 at the age of ninety! Maurice Koechlin's descendants are still alive today. Some of them include the famous Bollywood actress Kalki Koechlin, born in 1984, who is an Indian actress. She has received two of India's highest-ranking awards in film, the National Film Award and the Filmfare Award. Her movies are worth checking out if you want to look at the Koechlin family further. Another descendant is Paul Koechlin, 1852 to 1907, who was the winner of one of the earliest automobile races in the world, the *Paris-Bordeaux-Paris* race. Another interesting Paul was Paul Koechlin (Paul is one of the four most commons names in France, the second is Victor), 1881 to 1916, who was actually the nephew of the first Paul, and was a pioneer for aviation. He created his first plane in 1908 and had an aviation school in Paris.

The Koechlin family are quite interesting, aren't they?

Gustave Eiffel is our main character, our *Pièce de résistance* if you will. Not much is known about his family life, other than the fact that he was married, and had three daughters and two sons. History remembers him more for his engineering and architectural feats. Such as the Eiffel Tower, the internal structure of the Statue of Liberty, and the Bordeaux Bridge, Eiffel's first work. His greatest work was indeed the Eiffel Tower. The headlines in the novel are taken from real newspapers in the time period, and the Committee of Three Hundred was a very real thing, a hard push back against the project. The names on the side of the Tower, if you have not figured it out by now, is where the novel's title comes from. The Tower has the names on the top of the first level — seventy-two around the entire structure — very wonderful to look at and extremely intriguing. Charles Garnier is also historically correct, as he was leading the Committee at the time. He's also worth a Google, if you are so interested.

Any coincidences of there being an actual Aleron Arago are purely coincidental, he as well as Clarisse, Alex, Val, and Tomas, and most of the characters are fictional. Those that are not, are based *very* loosely on their real counterparts.

174

Again, thank you so much for choosing this story, it was a wonder to write it and put the time in to do research for it. I hope you loved the novel!

Tout mon amour,

S.F.Brooke

Acknowledgments

Let me say thank you first off to my Lord, that He gave me the right group of people to make this novel a reality, the willpower, imagination, and the time to bring it to life.

Second, thank you Ms. Ortega for her wonderful class and encouragement throughout the semester. I did it! I actually completed it like I said I would! I hope that you enjoy the novel.

Third, thank you to all of my friends and my sister who read a lot of rough drafts of this thing, Dr. Zarkov (you know who you are), and my parents who were willing to sit and listen as I brainstormed and asked more times that I could count if the story was good enough. Thank you to everyone who was interested in the creations of this book and kept asking when it was finally going to be published. Thank you all for the encouragement and the motivation to keep me writing. Good job you guys!

Thank you to my editing staff who caught all of my mistakes and were willing to spend the time to correct each paper.

I couldn't do this without all of you!